Honey and the Hired Hand

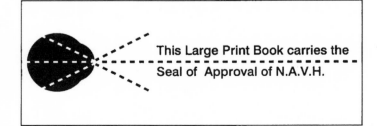

Honey
and the
Hired Hand

Joan Johnston

Thorndike Press • Waterville, Maine

Published in 2005 by arrangement with
Harlequin Books S.A.

Thorndike Press® Large Print Americana.

The tree indicium is a trademark of Thorndike Press.

The text of this Large Print edition is unabridged.
Other aspects of the book may vary from the original edition.

Set in 16 pt. Plantin by Myrna S. Raven.

Printed in the United States on permanent paper.

Library of Congress Cataloging-in-Publication Data

Johnston, Joan, 1948–
    Honey and the hired hand / by Joan Johnston.
        p. cm.
    ISBN 0-7862-7292-9 (lg. print : hc : alk. paper)
    1. Widows — Fiction.   2. Cowboys — Fiction.
    3. Women ranchers — Fiction.   4. Single mothers —
Fiction.   5. Cattle stealing — Fiction.   6. Undercover
operations — Fiction.   7. Large type books.   I. Title.
PS3560.O3896H66 2005
    813′.54—dc22   2004024863

For my friends,
Sally, Sherry and Heather —
the Square Table at JJ's

As the Founder/CEO of NAVH, the only national health agency solely devoted to those who, although not totally blind, have an eye disease which could lead to serious visual impairment, I am pleased to recognize Thorndike Press★ as one of the leading publishers in the large print field.

Founded in 1954 in San Francisco to prepare large print textbooks for partially seeing children, NAVH became the pioneer and standard setting agency in the preparation of large type.

Today, those publishers who meet our standards carry the prestigious "Seal of Approval" indicating high quality large print. We are delighted that Thorndike Press is one of the publishers whose titles meet these standards. We are also pleased to recognize the significant contribution Thorndike Press is making in this important and growing field.

Lorraine H. Marchi, L.H.D.
Founder/CEO
NAVH

★ Thorndike Press encompasses the following imprints: Thorndike, Wheeler, Walker and Large Print Press.

One

The hairs prickled on the back of Honey
Farrell's neck. She was being watched.
Again. Surreptitiously she scanned the room
looking for someone — anyone — she could
blame for the disturbing sensation that had
plagued her all evening. But everyone in the
room was a friend or acquaintance. There
was no one present who could account for
the eerie feeling that troubled her.

Her glance caught on the couple across
the room from her. How she envied them!
Dallas Masterson was standing behind his
wife, his hands tenderly circling Angel's
once-again-tiny waist. Their three-month-
old son was asleep upstairs. Honey felt her
throat close with emotion as Dallas leaned
down to whisper into his wife's ear. Angel
laughed softly and a pink flush rose on her
cheeks.

Honey saw before her a couple very
much in love. In fact, she had come to the
Mastersons' home this evening to help
them celebrate their first wedding anniversary. Honey found it a bittersweet event.
For, one year and one month ago, Honey's

husband, Cale, had been killed saving Dallas Masterson's life.

Honey felt her smile crumbling. A watery sheen blurred her vision of the Texas Rangers and their wives chattering happily around her. Mumbling something incoherent, she shoved her wineglass into the hands of a startled friend.

"Honey, are you all right?"

"I just need some air." Honey bit down on her lower lip to still its quiver as she hastened from the living room.

The overhead light in the kitchen was blinding, and Honey felt exposed. Shying from the worried look of another Ranger's wife, who was putting a tray of canapés into the oven, Honey shoved her way out the back screen door.

"Honey?" the woman called after her. "Is something wrong?"

Honey forced herself to pause on the back porch. She turned back with a brittle smile and said, "I just need some air. I'll be fine."

The woman grinned. "I suppose it's all the speculation about you and Adam Philips. Has he proposed yet? We're expecting an announcement any day."

Honey gritted her teeth to hold the smile in place, hoping it didn't look as much like a grimace as it felt. "I — could we talk about this later? I really do need some air."

She waited until the other woman nodded before pulling the wooden door closed behind her, abruptly shutting out the noise and the painful, though well-intentioned, nosiness of her friends and neighbors.

The early summer evening was blessedly cool with a slight breeze that made the live oaks rustle overhead. Honey sank onto the back porch steps. She leaned forward and lifted the hair off her nape, shivering when the breeze caught a curl and teased it across her skin as gently as a man's hand.

She quickly dropped her hair and clutched her hands together between her knees. She felt bereft. And angry. *How could you have left me alone like this, Cale? I'm trying to forget what it was like to be held in your arms. I'm trying to forget the feel of your mouth on mine.* But seeing Angel in Dallas's arms tonight had been a vivid reminder of what she had lost. And it hurt. It was hard to accept Cale's untimely death and go on with her life. But she was trying.

At least she had learned from her mistake. She would never again love a man who sought out danger the way Cale had. She would never again put herself in the position of knowing that her husband welcomed the risks of a job that might mean his death. Next time she would choose a man who would be there when she needed him. Inevitably Cale had been gone on some assignment for the Texas Rangers whenever a crisis arose. Honey had become adept over the years at handling things on her own.

If her friends and neighbors got their wish, she wouldn't be on her own much longer. Only this time she had chosen more wisely. The man who had brought her to the party tonight, Adam Philips, was a country doctor. Adam would never die from an outlaw's bullet, the way Cale had. And Adam was reliable. Punctual almost to a fault. She would be able to count on him through thick and thin.

That was a definite plus in weighing the decision she had to make. For the good-natured gossip at the party about her and the young doctor was founded in fact. Adam Philips had proposed to her, and Honey was seriously considering his offer. Adam was a handsome, dependable man in a safe occupation. He liked her sons, and they liked — perhaps *tolerated* was a better word to describe how they felt about him. There was only one problem.

Honey didn't love Adam.

Maybe she would never love another man the way she had loved Cale. Maybe she was hoping for too much. Maybe it would be better to marry a man she didn't love. That way her heart could never be broken again if —

The kitchen door rattled behind her. Afraid that someone would find her sitting alone in the dark and start asking more awkward questions, Honey rose and headed toward the corner of the house where the spill of light from the kitchen windows didn't reach. She almost ran into the man before she realized he was there.

He was leaning against Dallas's Victorian house, his booted foot braced against the painted wooden wall, his Stetson tipped forward over his brow so his face was in deep shadow. His thumbs were stuck into the front of his low-slung, beltless jeans. He was wearing a faded western shirt with white piping and pearl snaps that reflected the faint light of a misted moon.

Honey felt breathless. She wasn't exactly frightened, but she was anxious because she didn't recognize the man. He might have been a party guest, but he wasn't dressed for a party. He looked more like a down-on-his-luck cowboy, a drifter. It was better not to take a chance. Honey slowly backed away.

With no wasted movement, the cowboy reached out a hand and caught her wrist. He didn't hold her tightly, but he held her, all the same.

Honey stood transfixed by the feel of his callused fingers on her flesh. "I'll scream if you don't let go," she said in a miraculously calm voice.

The cowboy grinned, his teeth a white slash in the darkness. "No you won't."

There was a coiled tension in the way he held his body that she recognized. Cale had been like that. Ready to react instantly to any threat. Suddenly her curiosity was greater than her fear. She stopped straining against his hold. Instantly his grasp loosened, but he didn't let go.

"I've been standing out on the front porch watching you through the window, waiting for a chance to talk to you," the drifter said.

So, she wasn't crazy. Someone *had* been watching her all evening. His eyes weren't visible beneath the brim of his hat, but she felt the hairs rise on her nape. He was watching her right now. She ignored the gooseflesh that rose on her arms as he caressed her wrist with his thumb.

"I'm listening," she said. Regrettably the calm was gone from her voice.

"I know you're having some trouble handling things all by yourself at the ranch and —"

"How could you possibly know what's going on at the Flying Diamond?"

"Dallas told me how things are with you."

She exhaled with a loud sigh. "I see." He was no stranger then, although just who he was remained a mystery.

"It wouldn't have been hard to tell you've got problems just by looking at you."

"Oh? Are you some kind of mind reader?"

"No. But I can read people."

She remained silent, so he continued, "That frown never left your brow all evening."

Honey consciously relaxed the furrows of worry on her brow.

"Judging from the purple shadows I saw under your eyes, you aren't sleeping too well. You aren't eating much, either. That dress doesn't fit worth beans."

Honey tugged at the black knit dress she was wearing. Undeniably she had lost

13

weight since Cale's death.

"Not that I don't like what I see," the cowboy drawled.

Honey felt a faint irritation — laced with pleasure — when his grin reappeared.

"You're long legged as a newborn filly and curved in all the right places. That curly hair of yours looks fine as corn silk, and your eyes, why I'd swear they're blue as a Texas sky, ma'am."

Honey was mortified by her body's traitorous reaction as his eyes made a lazy perusal of her face and form. She felt the heat, the anticipation — and the fear. She recognized her attraction to the man even as she fought against it. This tall, dark-eyed drifter would never be reliable. And he had *danger* written all over him.

"Who are you?" Her voice was raspy and didn't sound at all like her own.

"Jesse Whitelaw, ma'am." The drifter reached up with his free hand and tugged the brim of his Stetson.

The name meant nothing to her; his courtesy did nothing to ease her concern. She stared, waiting for him to say why he had sought her out, why he knew so much about her when she knew nothing about him.

He stared back. She felt the tension grow

between them, the invisible electrical pulse of desire that streaked from his flesh to hers. Unconsciously she stepped back. His hold on her wrist tightened, keeping her captive.

His voice was low and grated like a rusty gate. "Dallas told me about your husband's death. I came here tonight hoping to meet you."

"Why?"

"I need a job."

The tension eased in Honey's shoulders. She released a gust of air she hadn't realized she'd been holding. Despite what he'd said, the way he'd looked at her, he hadn't sought her out to pursue a physical relationship. She couldn't help the stab of disappointment, when what she ought to feel was relief. At least now she knew how to deal with him.

"I can't afford to hire anyone right now," she said. "Especially not some down-on-his-luck drifter."

The smile was back. "If I wasn't down on my luck, I wouldn't need the job."

She couldn't hire him, but she was curious enough about him to ask, "Where did you work last?"

His shoulders rolled in a negligent shrug. "I've been . . . around."

"Doing what?" she persisted.

"A little cowboying, some rodeo bull riding, and . . . some drifting."

Bull riding. She should have known. Even Cale had never ridden bulls because he had thought it was too dangerous. *Drifting.* He was a man who couldn't be tied to any one place or, she suspected, any one woman. The last thing she needed at the Flying Diamond was a drifting cowboy who rode bulls for fun. Not that she could afford to hire him, anyway.

Just today she had discovered over fifty head of cattle missing — apparently rustled — from the Flying Diamond. That loss would cut deep into the profits she had hoped to make this year. "I can't hire anyone right now," she said. "I —"

The back door opened, revealing the silhouette of a large man in the stream of light. "Honey? Are you out here?"

She recognized Dallas, who was joined at the door by Angel.

"Are you coming in?" Dallas asked Honey.

"Yes. Yes, I am." She took advantage of Dallas's interruption to slip from the drifter's grasp. But he followed her. She could feel him right behind her as she stepped onto the porch.

Honey turned to the stranger to excuse herself and gasped. The harsh light from the kitchen doorway revealed the man's features. She was suddenly aware of his bronzed skin, of the high, broad cheekbones, the blade of nose and thin lips that proclaimed his heritage.

"You're Indian!" she exclaimed.

"The best part of me, yes, ma'am."

Honey didn't know what to say. She found him more appealing than she cared to admit, yet the savage look in his eyes frightened her. To her dismay, the drifter put the worst possible face on her silence.

His lips twisted bitterly, his grating voice became cynical as he said, "I suppose I should have mentioned that my great-grandfather married a Comanche bride. If it makes a difference —"

Honey flushed. "Not at all. I was just a little surprised when I saw . . . I mean, I didn't realize . . ."

"I'm used to it," he said. From the harsh sound of his voice it was clear he didn't like it.

Honey wished she had handled the situation better. She didn't think any less of him because he was part Indian, even though she knew there were some who would. She turned back to Angel and saw

17

that the young woman had retreated into the safety of Dallas's arms.

"I came outside for some air," Honey explained to Dallas. "And I met someone who says he's a friend of yours."

Dallas propelled Angel ahead of him onto the back porch and pulled the kitchen door closed behind him. "Hello, Jesse. I wasn't expecting you tonight."

Jesse shrugged again. "I got free sooner than I thought I would. Anyway, I could have saved myself the trip. Mrs. Farrell says she can't afford to hire anyone right now."

Dallas pursed his lips in disapproval. "I don't think you can afford not to hire someone, Honey."

"I'm not saying I don't need the help," Honey argued. "I just don't have the money right now to —"

"Who said anything about money?" Jesse asked. "I'd work for bed and board."

Honey frowned. "I really don't —"

"If you're worried about hiring a stranger, I'll vouch for Jesse," Dallas said. "We went to Texas Tech together."

"How long ago was that?" Honey asked.

"Fifteen years," Dallas admitted. "But I'd trust Jesse with my life."

Only it wouldn't be Dallas's life that

18

would be at stake. It was Honey's, and those of her sons, Jack and Jonathan. "I'll think about it," she said.

"I'm afraid I need something a little more definite than that," Jesse said. He tipped his hat back and said, "A drifting man needs a reason to light and set, or else he just keeps on drifting."

Honey didn't believe from looking at him that Jesse Whitelaw would ever settle anywhere for very long. But another pair of hands to share the load, even for a little while, would be more than welcome. There was some ranch work too heavy for her to handle, even with her older son's help. Honey brushed aside the notion that she would be alone with a stranger all day while the boys were at school. It was only a matter of weeks before her sons would be home for summer vacation.

She took a deep breath and let it out. "All right. When can you start?"

"I've got some things to do first."

Honey felt a sense of relief that she wouldn't have to face him again in the near future. It evaporated when he said, "How about bright and early tomorrow morning?"

Honey sought a reason to keep him away a little longer, to give herself some time to reconsider what she was doing, but nothing came to mind. Anyway, she needed the help now. There was vaccinating to be done, and she needed to make a tally of which cattle were missing so she could make a more complete report to the police.

Also she needed to add some light to improve security around the barn where she kept General, the champion Hereford bull that was the most important asset of the Flying Diamond.

"Tomorrow morning will be fine," she said.

The words were barely out of her mouth when the kitchen door was thrust open and another silhouette appeared. "I've been looking everywhere for you. What are you doing out here?"

Adam Philips joined what was quickly becoming a crowd on the back porch. He strode to Honey's side and slipped a possessive arm around her waist. "I'm Adam Philips," he said by way of introduction to the stranger he found there. "I don't think we've met."

"Jesse Whitelaw," the stranger said.

Honey watched as the two men shook hands. There was nothing cordial about the greeting. She didn't understand the reason for the animosity between them; it existed nonetheless.

"Are you ready to come back inside?" Adam asked.

He had tightened his hold on her waist until it was uncomfortable. Honey tried to step out of his grasp, but he pulled her back against his hip.

"I think the lady wants you to let her go," Jesse said.

"I'll be the judge of what the lady wants," Adam retorted.

The drifter's eyes were hard and cold, and Honey felt sure that at any moment he would enforce his words with action. "Please let go," she said to Adam.

At first Adam's grip tightened, but when he glanced over at her, she gave him a speaking look that said she meant business. Reluctantly he let her go.

"It's about time we headed home, don't you think?" Adam said to Honey.

Honey was irked by Adam's choice of words, which insinuated that they lived together. However, she didn't think now was the moment to take him to task. The drifter was still poised for battle, and Honey didn't want to be the cause of any more of a scene than had already occurred.

"It is getting late," she said, "and I've got

a long day tomorrow. It was nice meeting you, Jesse. I'll see you in the morning."

Honey anticipated Adam's questions and hurried him back inside. It took them a while to get through the kitchen, which now held several women collecting leftover potluck dishes to be carried home.

"Aha! I expect you two were out seeing a little of the moonlight," one teased.

"We'll be hearing wedding bells soon," another chorused.

Honey didn't bother denying their assumptions. They might very well prove true. But it was hard to smile and make humorous rejoinders right now, because she was still angry with Adam for his caveman behavior on the back porch.

When they reached the living room, a Randy Travis ballad was playing. "Dance with me?" Adam asked. His lips curved in the charming smile that had endeared him to her when they first met. Right now it wasn't doing a thing to put her in a romantic mood. However, it would be harder to explain her confused feelings to Adam than it would be to dance with him. "Sure," she said, relenting with a hesitant smile.

At almost the same moment Adam took her into his arms, she spied the drifter entering the living room. He stayed in the shadows, but Honey knew he was there. She could feel him watching her. She stiffened when Adam's palm slid down to the lowest curve in her spine. It wasn't something he hadn't done before. In the past, she had permitted it. But now, with the drifter watching, Adam's possessive touch felt uncomfortable.

Honey stepped back and said, "I'm really tired, Adam. Do you think we could go now?"

Adam searched her face, looking for signs of fatigue she knew he would find. "You do look tired," he agreed. "All right. Do you need to get anything from the kitchen?"

"I'll pick up my cake plate another time," she said. She felt the drifter's eyes on her as Adam ushered her out the front door to his low-slung sports car. He opened the door for her and she slid inside. Protected by the darkness within the car she was able to look back toward the house without being observed. She felt her nape prickle when she caught sight of the drifter standing at the front window.

Honey knew he couldn't see her, yet she felt as though his eyes pinned her to the seat. They were dark and gleamed with some emotion she couldn't identify. She abruptly turned away when Adam opened the opposite door and the dome light came on.

Adam put a country music tape on low, setting a romantic mood which, before Honey had met the drifter, she would have appreciated. Right now the mellow tones only agitated her, reminding her that Adam had proposed and was waiting for her answer. He expected her to give him a decision tonight. To be honest, she had led him to believe her answer would be yes. They hadn't slept together; she hadn't been ready to face that kind of intimacy with another man. But she had kissed him, and it had been more than pleasant.

"Honey?"

"What?" Her voice was sharp, and she cleared her throat and repeated in a softer tone, "What?"

"Are you sure you want to hire that drifter?"

"I don't see that I have much choice. There's work to be done that I can't do myself."

"You could marry me."

The silence after Adam spoke was an answer in itself. Honey knew she shouldn't give him hope. She ought to tell him right

24

now that she couldn't marry him, that it wasn't right to marry a man she didn't love. But the thought of that drifter, with his dark, haunting eyes, made her hold her tongue. She was too attracted to Jesse Whitelaw for her own good. If she were free, she might be tempted to get involved with him. And that would be disastrous.

But was it fair to leave Adam hanging?

Honey sighed. It seemed she had sighed more in the past evening than she had in the past year. "I can't —"

"You don't have to give me your answer now," Adam said. "I know you still miss Cale. I can wait a little longer. Now that you have that hired hand, it ought to make things easier on you."

They had arrived at the two-story wood frame ranch house built by Cale's grandfather. Adam stopped his car outside the glow of the front porch light. He came around and opened the door and pulled her out of the car and into his arms.

Honey was caught off guard. Even so, as Adam's lips sought her mouth she quickly turned aside so he kissed her cheek instead.

Adam lifted his head and looked down at her, searching her features in the shadows. Something had changed between them tonight. He thought of the stranger he had found with Honey on the Mastersons' back porch and felt a knot form in his stomach. He had always known that his relationship with Honey was precarious. He had hoped that once they were married she would come to love him as much as he loved her. He hadn't counted on another man coming into the picture.

Honey kept her face averted for a moment longer but knew that was the coward's way out. She had to face Adam and tell him what she was feeling.

"Adam, I —"

He put his fingertips on her lips. "Don't say anything. Just kiss me good night, and I'll go."

Honey looked up into his eyes and saw a tenderness that made her ache. Why didn't she love this man? She allowed his lips to touch hers and it was as pleasant as she remembered. But when he tried to deepen the kiss, she backed away.

"Honey?"

"I'm sorry, Adam. It's been a long day."

He looked confused and even a little hurt. But she had tried twice to refuse his proposal and he hadn't let her do it. Maybe her response to his kiss had told him what she hadn't said in words. Then he smiled, and she could have cried because his words were thoughtful, his voice tender. "Good night, Honey. Get some rest. I'll call you next week."

He would, too. *Good old reliable Adam.* She was a fool not to leap at the chance to marry such a man.

Honey stood in the shadows until he was gone. When she turned toward the house she saw the living room curtain drop. That would be her older son, Jack. He kept an eagle eye on her, which hadn't helped Adam's courtship. She called out to him as she unlocked the door and stepped inside.

"Come on down, Jack. I know you're still awake."

The lanky thirteen-year-old ambled back down the stairs he had just raced up. "He didn't stay long," Jack said. "You tell him no?"

"I haven't given him an answer."

"But you're going to say no, right?"

She heard the anxiety in Jack's voice. He wasn't ready to let anyone in their closed circle and most certainly not a man to take his father's place. She didn't dare tell him how she really felt before she told Adam, because her son was likely to blurt it out at an inopportune moment. She simply said,

27

"I haven't made a decision."

Honey put an arm around her son's shoulder and realized he was nearly as tall as she was. *Oh, Cale. I wish you could see how your sons have grown!* "Come on," she said. "Let's go make some hot chocolate."

"I'd rather have coffee," Jack said.

She arched a brow at him. "Coffee will keep me awake, and I need all the rest I can get."

Jack eyed her and announced somberly, "School will be out in about three weeks, Mom. I don't think I can do any more around here until then."

"You don't have to," she said. "I've hired a man to help out."

"I thought we couldn't afford hired help."

"He'll be working for room and board."

"Oh. What's he like?"

Honey wasn't about to answer that question. She couldn't have explained how she felt about the drifter right now. "He'll be here in the morning and you can ask him all the questions you want."

From the look her son gave her, she suspected Jack would grill the drifter like a hamburger. She smiled. That, she couldn't wait to see.

Jesse Whitelaw had another big surprise coming if he harbored any notions of pursuing Honey on her home ground. Her teenage son was a better chaperon than a Spanish duenna.

Two

Honey yawned and stretched, forcing the covers off and exposing bare skin to the pre-dawn chill. She scooted back underneath the blanket and pulled it up over her shoulders. She was more tired than she ought to be first thing in the morning, but she hadn't slept well. For the first time in over a year, however, it wasn't memories of Cale that had kept her awake.

The drifter!

Honey bolted upright in her bed. He was supposed to show up bright and early this morning. She glanced out the lace curtains in her upstairs bedroom and realized it was later than she'd thought. Her sons would already be up and getting ready for school. She tossed the covers away, shivering again as the cold air hit flesh exposed by her baby doll pajamas. She grabbed Cale's white terry cloth robe and scuffed her feet into tattered slippers before hurriedly heading downstairs.

Halfway down, she heard Jonathan's excited voice. At eight he still sounded a bit squeaky. Jack's adolescent response was lower-pitched, but his voice occasionally broke when he least expected it. She was already in the kitchen by the time she realized they weren't talking to each other.

The drifter was sitting at the kitchen table, a cup of coffee before him. Honey clutched the robe to her throat, her mouth agape.

"Catch a lot of flies that way," the drifter said with a lazy grin.

Her jaws snapped closed.

"Good morning," he said, touching a finger to the brim of his Stetson.

"Is it?" she retorted.

His skin looked golden in the sunlight. There were fine lines around his eyes and deep brackets around his mouth that had been washed out by the artificial light the previous evening. He was older than she'd thought, maybe middle thirties. But his dark eyes were as piercing as she remembered, and he pinned her with his stare. Honey felt naked.

She gripped the front of the masculine robe tighter, conscious of how she was dressed — or rather, not dressed. She thrust a hand into her shoulder-length hair, which tumbled in riotous natural curls around her face. She wondered how her mascara had survived the night.

Usually it ended up clumped on the ends of her eyelashes or smudged underneath them. She reached up to wipe at her eyes, then stuck her hand in the pocket of the robe. It wasn't her fault he'd found her looking like something the cat dragged in.

Honey didn't want to admit that the real reason she resented this unsettling man's presence in her kitchen so early in the morning was that she hadn't wanted him to see her looking so . . . so mussed.

"What are you doing here?" she demanded.

He raised a brow as though the answer was obvious. And it was.

"I let him in," Jack said, his hazel eyes anxious. "You said the hired hand was coming this morning. I thought it would be okay."

Honey took several steps into the room and laid a hand on her older son's shoulder. "You did fine. I'm just a little surprised at how early Mr. Whitelaw got here."

"He said we can call him Jesse," Jonathan volunteered.

Honey bristled. The man had certainly made himself at home.

"Jesse helped me make my sandwich,"

Jonathan added, holding up a brown paper bag.

Honey's left hand curled into a fist in the pocket of the robe. "That was nice." Her voice belied the words.

"Jesse thinks I'm old enough to make my own lunch," Jonathan continued, his chest pumped out with pride.

Honey had known for some time that Jonathan could make his own sandwich, but she had kept doing it for him because the routine morning chore kept her from missing Cale so much. She was annoyed by the drifter's interference but couldn't say so without taking away from Jonathan's accomplishment.

"Jesse rides bulls and rodeo broncs," Jack said. "He worked last at a ranch in northwest Texas called Hawk's Way. He's gonna teach me some steer roping tricks. He's never been married but he's had a lot of girlfriends. Oh, and he graduated from Texas Tech with a degree in animal husbandry and ranch management."

It was hard for Honey not to laugh aloud at the chagrined look on Jesse's face as Jack recited all the information he'd garnered. The drifter had been, if not grilled, certainly a little singed around the edges.

The shoe was on the other foot as Jack

continued, "I told him how you haven't been coping too well since Dad — well, this past year. Not that you don't try," he backtracked when he spied the horrified look on his mother's face, "but after all, Mom, the work is pretty hard for you."

Honey was abashed by her son's forthrightness. "I've managed fine," she said. She didn't want Jesse Whitelaw thinking she needed him more than she did. After all, a drifter like him wasn't going to be around long. Soon enough she'd be managing on her own again.

She stiffened her back and lifted her chin. Staring Jesse Whitelaw right in the eye she announced, "And I expect I'll still be managing fine long after you've drifted on."

"The fact remains, you need me now, Mrs. Farrell," the drifter said in that rusty gate voice. "So long as I'm here, you'll be getting a fair day's work from me."

The silence that followed was uncomfortable for everyone except the younger boy.

In the breach Jonathan piped up, "Jesse thinks I should have a real horse to ride, not just a pony."

"I'm sure Jesse does," Honey said in as calm a voice as she could manage. "But

I'm your mother, and until I decide differently, you'll stick with what you have."

"Aww, Mom."

This was an old argument, and Honey cut it off at the pass. "The school bus will be here in a few minutes," she said. "You boys had better get out to the main road."

Honey gave Jonathan a hug and a quick kiss before he headed out the kitchen door. "Have a nice day, sweetheart."

Jack was old enough to pick up the tension that arced between his mother and the drifter. His narrowed glance leapt from her to Jesse and back again. "Uh, maybe I ought to stay home today. Kind of show Jesse around."

Honey forced herself to smile reassuringly. "Nonsense. You have reviews for finals starting this week. You can't afford to miss them. Jesse and I will manage fine. Won't we?"

She turned to Jesse, asking him with her eyes to add his reassurance to hers.

Jesse rose and shoved his chair under the table. "Appreciate the offer," he said to Jack. "But like your mom said, we'll be just fine."

"Then I better run, or I'll miss the bus." Jack hesitated another instant before he sprinted for the door. Honey would have

35

liked to hug Jack, too, but at thirteen, he resisted her efforts to cosset him.

A moment later they were alone. Jesse was watching her again, and Honey's body was reacting to the appreciation in his dark eyes. She rearranged the robe and pulled the belt tighter, grateful for the thick terry cloth covering. She felt the roses bloom on her cheeks and hurried over to the stove to pour herself a cup of coffee.

Too late she realized she should have excused herself to go upstairs to dress. If she left now without getting her coffee, he would know she was running scared. There was absolutely no reason for her to feel threatened. Dallas wouldn't have recommended Jesse Whitelaw if she had anything to fear from him. But she couldn't help the anxiety she felt.

"Would you like another cup of coffee?" she asked, holding up the pot.

"Don't mind if I do, Mrs. Farrell," Jesse said.

"Please, you might as well call me Honey."

"All right . . . Honey."

Her name sounded far more intimate in that rusty gate voice of his than she was comfortable with. She stared, mesmerized for a moment by the warmth in his dark eyes, then realized what she was doing and repeated her offer.

"More coffee?"

He brought his cup over, and she realized she had made another tactical error. She could actually feel the heat from his body as he stepped close enough for her to pour his coffee. She turned her back on him to pour a cup for herself.

"Those are fine boys you have." Jesse moved a kitchen chair and straddled it, facing her.

She leaned back against the counter rather than join him at the table. "In the future, I'd appreciate it if you don't come inside before I get downstairs," she said.

"I wouldn't have come in except Jack said you were expecting me."

"I was — that is — I didn't expect you quite so early."

That was apparent. Honey's bed-tossed hair and sleepy-eyed look made Jesse want to pick her up and carry her back upstairs. He wasn't sure what — if anything — she was wearing under the man's robe. From the way she kept tightening the belt and clutching at the neck of the thing, he was guessing it wasn't much. His imagination had her stripped bare, and he liked what he saw.

It was too bad about her husband. From what he'd heard, Cale Farrell had died a hero. He supposed a woman left alone to raise two kids wouldn't be thinking much about that. At least he was here to help her with the ranch work. Not that he would be around forever — or even for very long. But while he was here, he intended to do what he could to make her life easier.

He knew it would be easier for her if he didn't let her know he was attracted to her. But he wasn't used to hiding his feelings for a woman. The way he had been raised, part of respecting a woman was being honest with her. Jesse planned to be quite frank about his fascination with Honey Farrell.

He liked the way she'd prickled up last night, not at all intimidated by him. He liked the way she had stood her ground, willing to meet him eye to eye. He bristled when he thought of her with any other man — especially that Philips character. Jesse wasn't sure how serious their relationship was, but he knew Honey couldn't be in love with Philips. Otherwise she wouldn't have reacted so strongly to *his* touch.

At any rate, Jesse didn't intend to let the other man's interest in Honey keep him from pursuing her himself. Which wasn't going to be easy, considering her opinion of drifters in general, and him — a half-breed Comanche — in particular. His look was challenging as he asked, "What did you have in mind for me to do today?"

Honey had been watching Jesse's fingers trace the top rail of the wooden chair. There was a scar that ran across all four knuckles. She was wondering how he'd gotten it when his fist suddenly folded around the back of the chair. "I'm sorry — what did you say?"

"I asked what you wanted me to do today."

"There are some steers that need vaccinating, and the roof on the barn needs to be repaired. Some fence is down along the river and a few head of my stock have wandered onto the mohair goat ranch south of the Flying Diamond. I need to herd those strays back onto my land. Also —"

"That'll do for starters," Jesse interrupted. He rose and set his coffee cup on the table. "I'll start on the barn roof while you get dressed. Then we can vaccinate those steers together. How does that sound?"

Honey started to object to him taking charge of things, but she realized she was just being contrary. "Fine," she said. "I'll come to the barn when I'm dressed."

She waited for him to leave, but he just stood there looking at her. "What is it? Did I forget something?" she asked.

"No. I was admiring the view." He flashed a smile, then headed out the kitchen door.

Honey ran upstairs, not allowing herself time to contemplate the drifter's compliment. He probably didn't spend much time around respectable women. He probably didn't realize he shouldn't be blurting out what he was thinking that way. And she shouldn't be feeling so good about the fact the hired hand liked the way she looked.

She was grateful to discover that her mascara had been clumped, rather than smudged. She took the time to wash her face and reapply a layer of sun-sensitive makeup. It was a habit she'd gotten into and had nothing to do with the fact there was now a man around to see her. Honey dressed in record time in fitted Levi's, plaid western shirt, socks and boots.

Even so, by the time she reached the barn, Jesse was already on the roof, hammer in hand. He had his shirt off and she couldn't help looking.

Jesse had broad shoulders and a powerful chest, completely hairless except for a line of black down that ran from his navel into his formfitting jeans. His nipples provided a dark contrast to his skin, which looked warm to the touch. She could see the definition of his ribs above a washboard belly. His arms were ropy with muscle and already glistened with sweat. Here was a man who had done his share of hard work. Which made her wonder why he had never settled down.

It dawned on her that the drifter had chosen the most dangerous job to do first. He was standing on the peaked barn roof without any kind of safety rope as though he were some kind of mountain goat. How could he be so idiotically unconscious of the danger!

She started up the ladder he had laid against the side of the barn and heard him call, "No need for you to come up here."

She looked up and found him hanging facedown over the edge of the roof. "Be careful! You'll fall."

"Not likely," he said with a grin. "I grew up rambling around in high places."

"I suppose you had the top bunk in an upstairs bedroom," she said with asperity.

Jesse thought of the high canyon walls he had scaled as a youth on his family's northwest Texas ranch and grinned. "Let's just say I spent a lot of time climbing when I was a kid and leave it at that. By the way, I found the spot that needs to be patched. I brought the shingles up with me, but I didn't see hide nor hair of the roofing nails."

"I put them away. I'll get them for you." Honey headed back down the ladder and into the barn. As she passed General's stall, she patted the bull on the forehead. She and Cale had raised him from birth, and though he had a ring in his nose, he would have followed her around without it.

"Hi, old fella. Just let me get these nails for Jesse and I'll let you out in the corral for a while."

The barn was redolent with the odors of hay, leather and manure. Rather than hold her nose, Honey took a deep breath. There was nothing disagreeable to her about the smell of a ranch — or a hardworking man. Which made her think of the hired hand standing on the roof of her barn.

Honey didn't want to be charmed by Jesse Whitelaw, but there was no denying his charm. Maybe it was his crooked grin, or the way his eyes crinkled at the edges when he smiled, creating a sunburst of webbed lines. Or maybe it was the fact his dark eyes glowed with appreciation when he looked at her.

"Hey! Where are those nails?"

Honey jumped at the yell from above. "I'm getting them!" She grabbed the box of nails and headed back into the sunshine. Jesse had come to the edge of the roof and bent down to take the nails as she climbed the ladder and handed them up.

When he stood again, a trickle of sweat ran down the center of his chest. As Honey watched, it slid into his navel and back out again, down past the top button of his jeans. It was impossible to ignore the way the denim hugged his masculinity. It took a moment for Honey to realize he wasn't moving away. And another moment to realize he was aware of the direction of her gaze.

Honey felt a single curl of desire in her belly and a weak feeling in her knees. Her fingers gripped the ladder to keep from falling. She was appalled at the realization that what she wanted to do was reach out and touch him. She froze, unable to move farther up the ladder or back down.

"Honey?"

Jesse's voice was gruff, and at the sound of it she raised her eyes to his face. His lids were lowered, his dark eyes inscrutable.

She had no idea what he was thinking. His jaw was taut. So was his body. Honey was afraid to look down again, afraid of what she would find.

She felt her nipples pucker, felt the rush of heat to her loins. Her lips parted as her breathing became shallow. Honey knew the signs, knew what they meant. And tried desperately to deny what she was feeling.

"Honey?" he repeated in a raw voice.

Jesse hadn't moved, but if possible, his body had tautened. His nostrils flared. She saw the pulse throb at his temple. What did he want from her? What did he expect? He was a stranger. A drifter. A man who loved danger.

She wasn't going to get involved with him. Not this way. Not any way. Not now. Not ever.

"No!" Honey felt as though she were escaping some invisible bond as she skittered down the ladder, nearly falling in her haste.

"Honey!" he shouted after her. "Wait!"

Honey hadn't thought he could get off the roof so fast, but she had no intention of waiting around for him. She started for the house on the run. She was terrified, not of the drifter, but of her own feelings. If he touched her . . .

Honey was fast, but Jesse was faster. He caught her just as she was starting up the front steps and followed her onto the shaded porch. When Jesse grabbed her arm to stop her, momentum slammed her body back around and into his. He tightened his arms around her to keep them both from falling.

Honey would have protested, except she couldn't catch her breath. It was a mistake to look up, because the sight of his eyes, dark with desire, made her gasp. Jesse captured her mouth with his. His hand thrust into the curls at her nape and held her head so she couldn't escape his kiss.

Honey wished she could have said she fought him. But she didn't. Because from the instant his lips took possession of hers, she was lost. His mouth was hard at first, demanding, and only softened as she melted into his arms. By then he was biting at her lips, his tongue seeking entrance. He tasted like coffee, and something else, something distinctly male. His kiss thrilled her, and she wanted more.

It was only when Honey felt herself pushing against Jesse that she realized he had spread his legs and pulled her into the cradle of his thighs. She could feel his arousal, the hard bulge that had caught her

45

unsuspecting attention so short a time ago. She heard a low, throaty groan and realized it had come from her.

Jesse's mouth mimicked the undulation of their bodies. Honey had never felt so alive. Her pulse thrummed, her body quickened. With excitement. With anticipation. *It had been so long.* She needed — craved — more. How could this stranger, this drifter, make her feel so much? Need so much?

At first Honey couldn't identify the shrill sound that interfered with her concentration.

Pleasure. Desire. Need.

The sound persisted, distracting her. Finally she realized it was the phone.

Honey hadn't been aware of her hands, but she discovered they were clutching handfuls of Jesse's black hair. His hat had fallen to the porch behind him. She stiffened. Slowly, she slid her hands away.

"The phone," she gasped, pushing now at his shoulders.

Honey felt Jesse's reluctance to release her. Whether he recognized the panic in her eyes, or the presumption of what he had done, he finally let her go. But he didn't step away. Honey had to do that herself.

"The phone," she repeated.

"You'd better answer it." It was clear he would rather she didn't. His body radiated tension.

Honey stood there another moment staring, her body alive with unmet needs, before she turned and raced inside the house. For a second she thought he would follow her, but from the corner of her eye she saw him whirl on his booted heel and head toward the barn.

She was panting by the time she snatched the phone from its cradle. "H-hello?"

"Honey? Why didn't you answer? Is everything all right?"

Dear Lord. It was Adam. Honey held her hand over the receiver and took several deep breaths, trying to regain her composure. There was nothing she could do about the pink spots on her cheeks except be grateful he wasn't there to see them.

At least there was one good thing that had come from the drifter's kiss. Honey knew now, without a doubt, that she could never marry Adam Philips. The sooner she told Adam, the better. Only she couldn't tell him over the phone. She owed him the courtesy of refusing him to his face.

"Honey, talk to me. What's going on?" Adam demanded.

"Everything's fine, Adam. I'm just a little breathless, that's all. I was outside when the phone started ringing," she explained.

"Oh. I called to see if your hired hand showed up."

"He's here."

There was a long pause. Honey wasn't about to volunteer any information about the man. If Adam was curious, he could ask.

"Oh," Adam said again.

To Honey's relief, it didn't appear he was going to pursue the subject.

"I know I said I wouldn't call until next week," he continued, "but an old school friend of mine in Amarillo called and asked me to come for a visit. His divorce is final and he needs some moral support. I'm leaving today and I don't know when I'll be back. I just wanted to let you know."

Good old reliable Adam. Honey rubbed at the furrow on her brow. "Adam, is there any chance you could come by here on your way out of town? I need to talk to you."

"I wish I could, but I'm trying to catch a flight out of San Antonio and it's going to be close if I leave right now. Can you tell me over the phone?"

"Adam, I —"

Honey felt the hair prickle on the back of her neck. She turned and saw that Jesse had stepped inside the kitchen door.

She stared at him helplessly. She swallowed.

"Honey? Are you still there?" Adam said.

"I'll see you when you get back, Adam. Have a good trip."

Honey hung up the phone without waiting to hear Adam's reply. She stared at Jesse, unable to move. He had put his shirt back on, but left it unsnapped so a strip of sun-warmed skin glistened down the middle of his chest. He had retrieved his Stetson and it sat tipped back off his forehead. His thumbs were slung into the front of the beltless jeans. He had cocked a hip, but he looked anything but relaxed.

"The repairs on the roof are done," he said. "I wanted to make sure it's all right with you if I saddle up that black stud to round up those steers that need vaccinating."

"Night Wind was Cale's horse," Honey said. "He hasn't been ridden much since —"

Naturally Jesse would want to ride the wildest, most dangerous horse in the stable. And why not? The man and the stallion were well matched.

"Of course, you can take Night Wind," she said. "If you wait a minute, I'll come with you."

"I don't think that's a good idea."

She didn't ask why not. He could use the distance and so could she. "All right," she said. "The steers that need to be vaccinated are in the west pasture. Come get me when you've got them herded into the corral next to the barn."

He tipped his hat, angled his mouth in that crooked smile and left.

Honey stared at the spot where he had been. She closed her eyes to shut out the vision of Jesse Whitelaw in her kitchen. It was plain as a white picket fence that she wasn't going to be able to forget the man anytime soon.

At least she had a respite for a couple of hours. She realized suddenly that because of Jesse's interruption she hadn't been able to refuse Adam's offer of marriage.

Horsefeathers!

She should never have kissed Jesse. Not that she had made any commitment to Adam, but she owed it to him to decline his offer before he found her in a compromising position with some other man. And not that she intended to get involved with Jesse Whitelaw, but so far, where that drifter was concerned, she hadn't felt as though things were under control. The smart move was to keep her distance from the man. That shouldn't be a problem. No problem at all.

Three

The black stud had more than a little buck in him, which suited Jesse just fine. He was in the mood for a fight, and the stud gave it to him. By the time the horse had settled down, Jesse had covered most of the rolling prairie that led to the west pasture. It wouldn't take long to herd the steers back to the chutes at the barn where they would be vaccinated. Only he had some business to conduct first.

Jesse searched the horizon and found what he was looking for. The copse of pecan trees stood along the far western border of the Flying Diamond. He rode toward the trees hoping that his contact would be there waiting for him. He spotted the glint of sun off cold steel and headed toward it.

"Kind of risky carrying a rifle around these parts with everyone looking out for badmen, don't you think?" Jesse said. He tipped his hat back slowly, careful to keep his hands in plain sight all the time.

"Don't know who you can trust nowadays," the other cowboy answered. "Your name Whitelaw?"

Jesse nodded. "From the description I got, you'd be Mort Barnes."

The cowboy had been easy to identify because he had a deep scar through his right eyebrow that made it look as if he had come close to losing his eye. In fact, the eye was clouded over and Jesse doubted whether Mort had any sight in it. The other eye was almost yellow with a black rim around it. Mort more than made up for the missing eye with the glare from his good one. Black hair sprouted beneath a battered straw cowboy hat and a stubble of black beard covered his cheeks and chin.

Jesse evaluated the other man physically and realized if he had to fight him, it was going to be a tooth and claw affair. The cowboy was lean and rangy from a life spent on horseback. He looked tough as rawhide.

"Tell your boss I got the job," Jesse said.

Mort smiled, revealing broken teeth. The man was a fighter, all right. "Yeah, I'll do that," Mort said. "How soon you figure you can get your hands on that prize bull of hers?"

"Depends. She keeps him in the barn. He's almost a pet. It won't be easy stealing him."

"The Boss wants —"

"I don't care what your boss wants. I do things my way, or he can forget about my help."

Mort scowled. "You work for the Boss, you take orders from him."

"I don't take orders from anybody. I promised I'd steal the bull for him and I will. But I do it my way, understand?" Jesse stared until Mort's one yellow eye glanced away.

"I'll tell the Boss what you said. But he ain't gonna like it," the cowboy muttered.

"If he doesn't like the way I do things he can tell me so himself," Jesse said. "Meanwhile, I don't want any more cattle stolen from the Flying Diamond."

The look in Mort's eye was purely malicious. "The Boss don't like bein' told what to do."

"If he wants that bull, he'll stay away from here. And tell him the next time one of his henchmen shows up around here he'd better not be carrying a gun."

Mort raised the rifle defensively. "I ain't ridin' around here without protection."

Jesse worked hard not to smile. It was pretty funny when the badman thought he needed a gun to protect himself from the good guys.

"Don't bring a gun onto the Flying Diamond again," Jesse said. "I won't tell you twice."

It was plain Mort didn't like being threatened, but short of shooting Jesse there wasn't much he could do. The outlaw had kept a constant lookout, so he spotted the rider approaching from the direction of the ranch house when there was no more than a speck of movement in the distance.

"You expectin' company?" Mort asked, gesturing toward the rider with his gun.

Jesse glanced over his shoulder and knew immediately who it was. "Dammit. I told her I'd come get her," he muttered. "It looks like Mrs. Farrell. Get the hell out of here and get now!"

Mort grinned. "Got plans of your own for the Missus, huh? Can't say as I blame you. Mighty fine lookin' woman."

Jesse grabbed hold of Mort's shirt at the throat and half pulled the man out of the saddle. The look in Jesse's eyes had Mort quailing even though the outlaw was the one with the gun. "That's no way to talk about a lady, Mort."

The outlaw swallowed hard. "Didn't mean nothin' by it."

Jesse released the man's shirt. He

straightened it with both hands, carefully reining his temper. "Back up slow and easy and keep that rifle out of the sunlight. No sense me having to make explanations to Mrs. Farrell about what you're doing here."

Mort wasn't stupid. What Jesse said made sense. Besides, the Boss would skin him alive if he got caught anywhere near Mrs. Farrell. "I'm skedaddlin'," he said.

Without another word, Mort backed his horse into the copse of pecans and out of sight. Jesse whirled the stud and galloped toward Honey to keep her from coming any closer before Mort made good his escape.

Why hadn't she waited for him at the ranch, as he'd asked? Damned woman was going to be more trouble than he'd thought. But she was sure a sight for sore eyes.

Her hair hung in frothy golden curls that whipped around her head and shoulders as she cantered her bay gelding toward him. She ought to be wearing a hat, he thought. As light-skinned as she was, the sun would burn her in no time at all. He remembered how her pale hand had looked in his bronzed one, how soft it had felt between his callused fingers and thumb. Never had he been more conscious of who and what he was.

Jesse hadn't known at first what it meant to be part Indian. He had learned. *Breed. Half-breed. Dirty Injun.* He had heard them all. What made it so ironic was the fact that neither of his two older brothers, Garth and Faron, nor his younger sister, Tate, looked Indian at all. He was the only one who had taken after their Comanche ancestors.

His brothers hadn't understood his bitterness at being different. They hadn't understood the cause for his bloody knuckles and blackened eyes. Surprisingly, it was his half-English, half-Irish father who had made him proud he was descended from a warrior people, the savage Comanche.

That knowledge had shaped his whole life.

Jesse had often wondered what would have happened if he had been born a hundred years earlier; he often felt as barbaric as any Comanche. He had not been able to settle in one place, but needed to wander as his forebears had. While it was still a ruthless world he lived in, the conventions of society had glossed over the ugliness so it was not as apparent. Except, he had chosen a life that brought him into daily contact with what was cruel and sordid in the modern world. And forced him daily to confront his own feral nature.

Jesse no longer apologized for who and what he was. He had not tied himself to any one place, or any one person. He had never minded being alone or even considered the loneliness and isolation caused by his way of life. Until he had met the woman riding toward him now.

His eyes narrowed on Honey Farrell. He wished he could tell her about himself. Wished he could explain how she made him feel, but he couldn't even tell her who he really was. Nevertheless, he had no intention of letting the circumstances keep them apart. It wasn't honorable to keep the truth from her, but he consoled himself with the thought that when this was all over, he would more than make it up to her.

It was unfortunate she didn't — couldn't — know the truth about him, but he convinced himself that it wouldn't matter to her. He would make her understand that they belonged together. And who — and what — he was would make no difference.

"Hello, there!" Honey called as she rode up to Jesse. "There was a phone call for you after you left."

Jesse took off his hat, thrust his hand through his too-long black hair and resettled the Stetson. "Can't imagine who'd call me," he said. His family had no idea where he was — and hadn't known for years.

"It was Dallas."

Jesse frowned. "Any particular reason for the call?"

"He invited you to dinner tonight." Honey didn't mention that Dallas had invited her to dinner as well. She had tried to refuse, but Dallas had put Angel on the phone, and Honey had succumbed to the other woman's plea for company.

Honey felt that same inexplicable tension she always felt around Jesse. Her gelding sidestepped and their knees brushed. That simple touch produced goose bumps on her arms. She was grateful for the long-sleeved Western shirt that hid her reaction. She stared off toward the copse of pecans in the distance, avoiding Jesse's startled glance.

And spotted a glint of sunlight off metal.

"There's someone in the trees behind you," Honey said in a quiet voice. "I think he has a gun."

Jesse said a few pithy words under his breath. "Don't let him know you see him.

59

Help me get these steers moving toward the barn."

"Do you think it might be one of the rustlers?" Honey asked as she loosened the rope from her saddle.

"Don't know and don't care," Jesse said. "That's a matter for the police. Best thing for us to do is get ourselves and these cattle out of here."

There was no discussion as they used whistles and an occasional slap with a lasso to herd the steers back toward the barn. When they were a safe distance away, Honey kneed her gelding over to join Jesse.

"I've lost a lot of stock to rustlers since Cale died," Honey said. "I suppose they don't believe I'm any threat to them. But I didn't think they'd dare let themselves be seen in broad daylight. I'll call the police when we get back to the house and —"

Jesse interrupted. "There's no need for that. I'll tell Dallas about it when I call to accept his dinner invitation."

Honey frowned. "I guess that'll be okay. Uh . . . I suppose I should have mentioned I've also been invited to dinner. Would you mind if I got a ride with you?"

Jesse kept the dismay he felt from his face. He had hoped to use the time he was away from the ranch to do some other business without Honey being any the wiser. Having her along meant he would have to curtail his plans. But he couldn't think of a good reason to refuse her a ride that wouldn't raise suspicion. "Sure," he said at last. "Why not? What time do you want to leave?"

"Around six, I suppose. That'll give me time after we finish with the vaccinating to get cleaned up and make some supper for Jack and Jonathan."

"That sounds fine. Meanwhile, until those rustlers are caught you'd better stay close to home."

Honey glanced at Jesse to see if he was serious. He was. "I have a ranch to run," she said.

"I'm here now. If there's work that needs to be done away from the house, I can do it."

"You're being ridiculous. I don't think —"

"No, you aren't thinking!" Jesse interrupted in a harsh voice. "What's going to happen if you chance onto those rustlers at the wrong time? They've killed before and —"

"Killed! Who? When?"

Jesse swore again. He hadn't meant to alarm her, just keep her safe. "A rancher near Laredo was found shot to death last month."

"Oh, my God," Honey whispered. "Surely it wasn't the same rustlers who took my cattle!"

"What if it is? Better safe than sorry. You stay around the ranch house." It came out sounding like the order it was.

Honey bristled. "I'm in charge here. And I'll do as I please!"

"Just try leaving," he said. "And we'll see."

"Why, of all the high-handed, macho cowboy talk I ever heard —"

Jesse grabbed the reins and pulled her gelding to a halt. "These guys aren't fooling around, Honey. They've killed once. They've got nothing to lose if they kill again. I wouldn't want anything to happen to you."

The back of his gloved hand brushed against her cheek. "I don't intend to lose you."

Honey's heart missed a beat. He was high-handed, all right, but when he spoke to her in that low raspy voice and looked at her with those dark mysterious eyes, she found herself ready to listen. Which made no sense at all.

"How does a drifter like you know so much about all this?" she asked.

"Dallas filled me in," he said. When she

still looked doubtful, he said, "Ask him yourself at dinner tonight."

"Maybe I will."

The entire time they vaccinated bawling cattle, Honey said nothing more about the dinner at Dallas Masterson's house. She was thinking about it, though, because she realized Jesse would have to use the upstairs bathroom to clean up. She had yet to explain to him that she planned for him to sleep in a room in the barn that hired hands had used in the past.

She decided to confront him before the boys got home from school, in case he decided to argue. They were both hot and sweaty from the work they'd been doing, so it was easy to say, "I could use some iced tea. Would you like some?"

"Sounds good," he replied. "I'll be up to the house in a minute. I have a few things to put away here first."

Honey was glad for the few moments the delay gave her to think about how to phrase what she wanted to say. She took her time in the kitchen, filling two glasses with ice and sun-brewed tea. She wasn't ready when he appeared at the screen door, hat in hand.

"May I come in?"

His request reminded her that she had

met Jesse Whitelaw less than twenty-four hours earlier. It seemed like a lot longer. Like maybe she had known the cowboy all her life. It left her feeling apprehensive. She avoided his eyes as she pushed the screen door wide and said, "Sure. I've made tea for both of us."

He moved immediately to the glass of tea on the table and lifted it to his lips. She watched as he tipped the glass and emptied it a swallow at a time. Rivulets of sweat streamed down his temples, and his hair was slick against his head where his hat had matted it down. He smelled of hardworking man, and she was all too aware of how he filled the space in her kitchen.

Jesse sighed with satisfaction as he set the empty glass on the table. The sound of the ice settling was loud in the silence that followed as his eyes found hers and held.

"I think I have time to look at whatever fence you have down before I have to get ready for supper," Jesse said. "If you'll just head me in the right direction."

"Certainly. There are a few things we need to discuss first." Honey threaded her fingers so she wouldn't fidget. "When I offered you room and board I wasn't thinking about where I'd put you. There's a room at the rear of the barn I can fix up for you, but you'll have to use the bathroom in the house."

Jesse worked to keep the grimace off his face. It would be a lot more difficult explaining how her prize bull had been stolen from the barn if he was sleeping there. "Are you sure there isn't somewhere in the house I could sleep? I don't need much."

Honey chewed on her lower lip. "There is a small room off the kitchen." She pointed out the closed door to him. "It's awfully tiny. I've started using it for a pantry. I don't think —"

Jesse opened the door and stepped inside. The room was long and narrow. Wooden shelves along one wall were filled with glass jars of preserves, most likely from the small garden he had seen behind the house. An iron bed with a bare mattress stood along the opposite wall under a gingham-curtained window. A simple wooden chest held a brass lamp and an old-fashioned pitcher and bowl for water.

"This'll do fine," he said.

"But —"

He turned and she was aware of how small the room was, or rather, how he filled it. She took a step back, away from the very strong attraction she felt. "The room in the barn is bigger," she argued.

"You'd have more privacy."

He grinned. "I suppose that's true, if you don't count the livestock."

"I have to come in here sometimes to get food from the shelves," she explained.

"You could knock."

"Yes, I suppose I could." It was hard to argue with logic. Yet Honey didn't want to concede defeat. Otherwise, she was going to find herself with the hired hand constantly underfoot. She made a last effort to convince him the barn was a better choice. "The boys sometimes make a lot of noise. Morning and evening. You won't get much peace and quiet if you stay here."

"I expect I'll be going to bed later and getting up earlier than they will," he replied.

Honey sighed. This wasn't working out as she had planned at all. Somehow she had ended up with this part-savage stranger, this drifter, living under her roof. She wasn't exactly frightened of him, but she was uneasy. After all, what did she really know about him?

He seemed to sense her hesitation and said, "If you don't feel comfortable with me in the house, of course I'll sleep in the barn."

There it was, her chance to avoid coping

with his presence in the house. She opened her mouth to say "Please do" and instead said, "That won't be necessary. I'm sure this will work out fine."

At that moment the kitchen screen door slammed open and Jonathan came racing through. "Hi, Mom! Hi, Jesse! I'm missing cartoons!" He was through the kitchen and gone before Honey could even gasp a hello.

A few moments later Jack appeared at the door. He didn't greet his mother or the hired man, simply dropped his books on the kitchen table and headed straight for the cookie jar on the counter. He reached inside and found it empty. "Hey! I thought you were going to bake some cookies today."

"I didn't have time," Honey apologized.

He opened a cupboard, looking for something else to eat.

Honey saw Jesse's jaw tighten, as though he wanted to say something but was biting his tongue. Perhaps Jack wasn't as courteous as he could have been, but from what Honey had gathered from the mothers of Jack's friends, it was typical teenage behavior. She was used to it. Apparently Jesse wasn't.

Jack seemed oblivious to them as he

hauled bread, peanut butter and jelly out onto the counter and made himself a sandwich.

Honey watched Jesse's expression harden. She wasn't sure whether to be more vexed and annoyed by Jack's conduct, or Jesse's reaction to it.

Jack picked up his sandwich, took a bite that encompassed nearly half of it, and headed out the kitchen door toward the den and the television.

"Do you have any homework?" Honey asked.

"Just studying for tests," Jack said through a mouthful of peanut butter. "I'll do it later."

Honey hadn't realized Jesse could move so fast. Before Jack reached the kitchen door, the hired hand blocked his way.

"Just a minute, son."

Jack stiffened. "You're in my way."

"That was the general idea."

Jack turned to his mother, clearly expecting her to resolve the situation.

Honey wasn't sure what Jesse intended, let alone whether she could thwart that intention. For her son's sake, she had to try. "Jesse —"

"This is between me and Jack," Jesse said.

"I don't have anything to say to you," Jack retorted.

"Maybe not. But I've got a few things to say to you."

Jack balled his fist, turning the sandwich into a squashed mess. "You've got no right —"

"First off, a gentleman greets a lady when he comes into the room. Second, he doesn't complain about the vittles. Third, he asks for what he needs from a lady's kitchen, he doesn't just take it. Fourth, he inquires whether chores need to be done before he heads for the bunkhouse. And finally, he doesn't talk with his mouth full."

Jack swallowed. The soft bread felt like spiny tumbleweed as it grated over the constriction in his throat. This was the kind of dressing-down his father might have given him. The kind of talking-to he hadn't had for more than a year, since his father's death. He resented it. Even though he knew deep down that the hired hand was right.

Jack angled his face to his mom, to see what she was going to do about the drifter's interference. He felt sick in the pit of his stomach when he saw how pale her face was. Jack turned from his mother and confronted the hired hand. He let the hostility he was feeling show in his eyes, but for his mother's sake, struggled to keep it out of his voice. "Maybe I was wrong," he conceded.

Jesse continued to stare at the boy and was pleased when the gangly teenager turned to his mother and gritted out, "Hello, Mom. Thanks for the sandwich."

Jack looked down at the mess in his hand and grimaced.

"You can wash your hands in the sink," Honey said.

Jesse stepped aside to allow the boy to pass and in doing so, glanced at Honey. Her dark blue eyes were afire with emotion, but it wasn't gratitude he saw there. Obviously he had stepped amiss. He clenched his teeth over the explanation for his actions that sprang to mind. She didn't look as though she wanted to hear reason.

Jesse and Honey stared at each other while Jack washed his hands. He turned from the sink, still drying his hands with a dish towel, and asked his mother, "Are there any chores that need to be done before supper?"

Since Cale's death, Honey had taken the responsibility for almost all the ranch chores her husband had done in the evening. When Jack offered, she realized there was work that still needed to be done in the barn that she would appreciate having Jack's help completing. "You can feed the stock," she said. "Also, I let General out into the corral. Would you bring him back inside the barn for the night?"

"Sure, Mom. Anything else?"

"That's all I can think of now."

Without looking at Jesse again, Jack pushed his way out the screen door and let it slam behind him.

The tension was palpable once the two adults were alone.

Jesse started to apologize for interfering, then bit his tongue. He had been hard on the boy, but no more so than his father had been with him. A tree grew as the sapling began. Now was the time for Jack to learn courtesy and responsibility.

"I don't quite know what to say," Honey began. "I don't agree with your methods, but I can't argue with the results. Maybe I've been too lax with Jack the past few months, but he took Cale's death so hard, I . . ."

Jesse heard the tremor in her voice and took a step toward her. As soon as he did, she squared her shoulders and lifted her chin.

"It hasn't been easy for any of us," she

said in a firmer voice. "But we've managed to get along."

Jesse heard "without your help" even though she didn't say the words. So be it. This was the last time he would get involved. If she wanted to let the boy walk all over her, that was her business. It was just fine with him.

Like hell it was.

"Look," he said. "I can't promise I won't say anything more to the boy. We have to work together, after all. But I'll try not to step on any toes in the future. How does that sound?"

"Like the best compromise I'm going to get," Honey replied with a rueful smile.

"Guess I'll go work on that fence."

"I'll take my bath early," she said. "That way the bathroom will be free when you get back."

"Fine."

He had to walk by her to get to the door. Honey marveled at how small any room got with the two of them in it. She stepped back until she pressed against the counter, but their bodies still brushed. Jesse hesitated just an instant before he continued past her. He didn't look back as he pushed his way out the screen door. But she noticed he caught the door and kept it from

72

slamming on his way out.

Honey heaved a sigh — of relief? — when she had the kitchen to herself again. She wished she didn't need Jesse's help so much on the ranch, because she wasn't at all sure she could handle having him around. His presence was already changing everything. She was beginning to feel things that she hadn't ever expected to feel again.

Nothing could come of her attraction to Jesse. He was a drifter. Sticking around wasn't in his nature. When the mood struck him, he would be moving on. And she would be left alone. Again.

She had best remember that when the yearning rose to let him get close.

Four

Honey scooted down, settled her nape on the edge of the free-standing, claw-footed bathtub and closed her eyes. Her entire body was submerged and steam rose from water that lapped at the top edge of the tub. There was no shower in the house, only this aged white porcelain tub. She smiled when she imagined what Jesse's reaction was going to be when he confronted this monstrosity.

It was easy to blame the absence of a modern shower on the lack of extra money over the years she and Cale had been married. But the truth was, Honey loved the old-fashioned deep-bellied tub, with its brass fixtures and lion's paw legs. Instead of putting in a shower, she and Cale had expanded the capacity of the water heater so it was possible to fill the giant tub with steaming hot water all the way to the top.

Honey had laced the scalding water with scented bath oil, and the room reeked of honeysuckle. She was reminded of hot baths she and Cale had taken together. Honey crossed her arms and caressed her shoulders, smoothing in the bath oil. And imagined how it would feel if Jesse . . .

Abruptly Honey sat up, sloshing water over the edge of the tub. Her eyes flew open and she looked around her. Her daydreams had seemed so real. For a moment it had seemed as though that man was here. In her tub. With her. His hands — never mind where his hands had been! And his mouth — Honey shivered in reaction to the vivid pictures her mind had painted.

"Horsefeathers!" she muttered.

Honey lunged up, splashing water on the floor, and grabbed for a terry cloth towel. She wrapped herself in it, then reached down to pull the plug. And felt a spurt of guilt. The water heater would fill the tub once — but not twice. Her remorse didn't last long, and a smile slowly appeared on her face. Jesse Whitelaw could stand to cool off a little. A nice cold bath ought to help him along.

Honey was in her bedroom and had almost finished dressing when Jesse knocked at her door.

"Hey, there's no shower in that bathroom," he said.

"I know." Honey tried to keep the grin out of her voice.

He muttered something crude under his

breath, then said, "Where are the towels?"

"The linens on the rack in the bathroom are yours to use."

Honey heard the water run for a short while, then stop. She left her bedroom and stood outside the bathroom door listening. There was a long silence, followed by a male yelp and frantic splashing. "This water's like ice!" he bellowed.

"I know," she said loud enough to be heard through the door. By now her grin was huge.

Jesse muttered again.

"I'm going downstairs to fix some dinner for Jack and Jonathan. Enjoy your bath."

Her laughter followed her down the stairs.

Jesse shivered, but not from the cold. It was the first time he'd heard Honey laugh, and the sound skittered down his spine. His lips curled ruefully. At least now he knew she had a sense of humor.

He soaped a rag and washed himself vigorously, as though that could obliterate his thoughts of her. But Honey Farrell had gotten under his skin. Every breath he took filled his lungs with the honeysuckle scent she had bathed in. Everywhere he looked there were reminders that he had invaded her feminine domain.

The pedestal sink was cluttered on top with all sorts of female paraphernalia — powder and lipstick and deodorant and suchlike — except where she had cleared a tiny space for his things.

Jesse cursed a blue streak as he rinsed himself with the icy water, then grabbed a towel and stepped out onto the deepest pile rug he had ever felt beneath his feet. It was decorated with whimsical daisies — as was the towel he had wrapped around his hips. If his brothers could see him now, they would rib him up one side and down the other.

He quickly pulled on clean briefs and jeans, then slung the towel around his neck while he shaved. He debated whether to leave his straight edge razor and strop in the bathroom, then decided that as long as she had left the space for him, he might as well use it. When he saw his things beside hers, he pursed his lips thoughtfully. It was as though an unfinished picture had been completed.

He spread the damp towel over the rack and put on the shirt he had brought into the bathroom with him. He had hoped the steam from a hot shower would ease some of the wrinkles out of it. Since he'd ended up taking a cold bath, he had no choice except to shrug into the wrinkled shirt.

Jesse started to borrow Honey's hair-brush but changed his mind and finger-combed his hair instead. It would hang straight once it dried no matter what he did with it now.

Jesse came down the stairs quietly and stood at the kitchen door undetected by the trio at the table. Honey was serving up her younger son's dinner. Her face was rosy, probably from all that hot water she'd bathed in, he thought with a silent chuckle. He was glad to see she wasn't wearing black again, but he thought the pale green was wrong for her.

She ought to be wearing vivid colors — reds and royal blues — that were as full of life as she was. He liked the way the dress clung to her figure, outlining her breasts and defining her slim waist and hips. She looked very much like a woman, and he felt the blood surge in his loins at the sight of her.

He watched unnoticed as Honey brushed a lock of hair off Jonathan's fore-head. She put a hand on Jack's shoulder as she set the salt and pepper before him. Then she found another reason to touch Jonathan. Jesse wondered if Honey had any idea what she was doing. He felt his body tauten with the thought of her touching him like that.

Jesse's family members were fiercely loyal to each other, but they weren't much for touching. He could count on one hand the number of times his mother had caressed him in any way. He hadn't realized until now just how needful he was of Honey's touch and the feel of her hands on his body.

"Oh, there you are!" Honey froze with her hand outstretched for the butter dish. She wondered how long Jesse had been standing there. He had a way of watching her that she found totally unnerving. His dark, hooded gaze revealed a hunger that took her breath away, but there was a yearning, almost wistful expression in his eyes as well.

"Are you ready to go?" he asked.

Honey took a good look at what the hired hand was wearing and frowned. She wondered what kind of life Jesse Whitelaw had led when this was all he had to wear to dinner. His jeans were clean but worn white at the stress points and seams. The faded western shirt was frayed at collar and cuffs and badly creased. His leather belt was dark with age and had a shiny silver buckle she felt sure he had earned as a prize at some rodeo. He wore the same tooled black leather boots he had worn all day; the scuff marks showed the hard use they'd had.

She almost offered to iron his shirt, then changed her mind. Somehow she knew he wouldn't appreciate the suggestion. Besides, if he had really been concerned about his appearance, he could have asked for the iron himself. "I'm ready anytime you are," she said.

The ride to Dallas's place in Jesse's pickup truck — which was barely two years old and in surprisingly good shape compared to his clothing — took barely an hour. Because of the long, uncomfortable silences between inane bits of conversation, it felt a lot longer.

Even in the modern West, a man was still entitled to his privacy. Thus Honey didn't feel she could ask Jesse about himself. That left a myriad of other subjects, not one of which came readily to mind.

The silence was deafening by the time Jesse said, "How long have you known Dallas and Angel?"

Honey grabbed at the conversational gambit like a gambler for a deck of cards. "I met Dallas about four years ago when he and Cale started working together on assignments for the Texas Rangers. Dallas introduced me to Angel a little over a year ago, about the same time she and Dallas met each other."

"How did the two of them meet?" Jesse asked.

"You know, they never said. Every time I asked, Angel blushed and Dallas laughed and said, 'You wouldn't believe me if I told you.'"

"How did you and that Philips guy meet?" Jesse asked.

That was more personal ground. Honey hesitated, then grinned and admitted, "Dallas invited me on a double date with Adam and Angel. By the end of the day, Dallas ended up with Angel, and Adam and I were a couple."

"How serious are things between you and Philips?"

Honey shot a quick look at Jesse, but his expression was bland. "I don't think that's any of your business."

"I think maybe it is."

"I can't imagine why —"

"Can't you?" His piercing gaze riveted her for a moment before he had to look at the road again.

Honey's pulse began to speed. She grasped at the opportunity to put the hired hand in his place once and for all. "Adam has asked me to marry him," she said.

A muscle jerked in Jesse's cheek. "You don't love him," he said curtly.

"You can't possibly know whether I love him or not."

He cocked a brow and his lips drew up cynically. "Can't I?"

Honey turned to stare out the window, avoiding his searching look.

"Are you going to marry him?"

"I —" Honey considered lying. Perhaps if she told Jesse she was committed to another man, he would leave her alone. But she couldn't use Adam like that — simply to keep another man at arm's length. "No," she admitted.

"Good."

Nothing else passed between them for the few minutes it took to traverse the length of the road from the cattle guard at the entrance to Dallas's ranch to the Victorian ranch house. At least, nothing in words. But Honey was aware of the portal the drifter had forced open between them.

"I won't ever hurt you," Jesse said in a quiet voice.

"You can, you know," she said in an equally quiet voice.

His lips flattened. "I don't want you to be afraid of me."

"Then leave me alone."

"I can't do that."

"Jesse . . ."

The Mastersons' porch light was on, and Jesse pulled the truck up well within its glow. He killed the engine and turned to look at Honey. "Is it your husband?" he asked bluntly.

Honey felt the pain that always came with memories of Cale. "Cale is dead."

"I know that. Do you?"

Honey gasped and turned to stare at Jesse. "What do you want from me?"

"More than it seems you're willing to give."

Jesse's sharp voice cut through her pain, and Honey realized she was angry. "You can hardly blame me," she said. "I'm not in a hurry to get my heart torn out again."

"Who says you have to?"

Honey snorted inelegantly. "That sounds pretty funny coming from a man like you. How many women have you loved and left, Jesse? How long should I plan on you hanging around? And what am I supposed to do when you're gone? I'd have to be a fool to get involved with you. And whatever else I might be, I'm no fool. I —"

Honey broke off when she saw Angel come running out onto the porch to greet them. She flashed Jesse a look of frustration and quickly stepped out of the truck and headed up the porch steps.

"It's good to see you again, Honey," Angel said as the two women hugged. She didn't offer her hand to the drifter and kept her distance. "Dallas is putting the baby to bed. He'll be down in a minute. Won't you both come inside?"

She stepped away from Jesse and held the door. Honey saw the other woman actually shiver as Jesse passed by her. Honey wondered what it was about the drifter that caused Angel to shy away from him. Was it possible that Dallas had told her something about Jesse? Something sinister?

Honey shook her head and dismissed the possibility. She didn't know much about Jesse, but she didn't see him as a villainous figure. Probably there was something in Angel's own past that was causing her to react so strangely to Dallas's friend.

Dallas had none of his wife's reservations. He greeted Jesse warmly and shook his hand. "I'm glad you could come on such short notice," Dallas said. "I thought maybe we could talk about old times, maybe get reacquainted. How are your brothers and your sister?"

Honey's eyes widened and she stared at Jesse as though she had never seen him before. "You have a family?"

Jesse grinned. "Two older brothers and a younger sister."

"Where?" Honey asked.

"At the family ranch, Hawk's Way, in northwest Texas near Palo Duro Canyon."

So, Jesse wasn't as much of a footloose drifter as he had led her to believe. He had some roots after all.

"Would anyone like something to drink?" Angel asked.

"Whiskey and water," Jesse said.

"Iced tea for me," Honey said.

"Dallas?"

"I'll join Jesse and have a whiskey, but without the water, Angel."

Honey sat on the Victorian sofa and Dallas took the leather chair that was obviously his favorite spot in the living room. Jesse joined Honey on the narrow sofa. It barely held the two of them, and Jesse's jean-clad leg brushed against her as he sat down.

Honey jerked away, then looked up to see if Dallas had noticed her reaction. He had. He looked concerned, but Honey wasn't about to explain the sexually fraught situation to him. Honey grimaced and folded her hands together in her lap. It was going to be a long evening.

Or it might have been if Angel hadn't been there. Honey had always liked Angel and had an affinity with the other woman that she couldn't explain. She did her best throughout the spicy Mexican meal to focus her attention on Angel and ignore Jesse Whitelaw. She wasn't totally successful.

It bothered Honey that Angel never got over her odd behavior around Jesse. Angel never quite relaxed, and her eyes were wary every time she looked at him. In fact, it bothered Honey enough that she mentioned it when she and Angel went upstairs to check on the baby after supper, leaving the men to stack the dishes in the dishwasher.

"You don't seem to like Jesse Whitelaw," Honey said bluntly.

Angel refused to meet her gaze, focusing instead on the baby sleeping in the crib. "It's not that I don't like him, it's just . . ."

"Just what? Has Dallas told you something about him? Something I should know?"

"Oh, no!" Angel reassured her. "It's nothing like that. It's just . . ."

Honey waited while Angel searched for the words to explain her aversion to the drifter.

"When I was much younger, I had a bad experience with some Indians." What Angel wasn't able to tell Honey was that she had seen the tortured remains of a Comanche raid in 1857. But no one except Dallas knew Angel had traveled through time to reach this century. So Angel was forced to explain how she felt without being able to give specific details.

"Whenever I look at Jesse," she said, "I see something in those dark eyes of his, something so savage, so feral, it reminds me of that time long ago. He terrifies me." Angel visibly shivered. "Aren't you afraid of him?"

"Sometimes," Honey admitted reluctantly. "But not in the way you are." Honey felt certain Jesse posed no physical threat to her. The wild, savage looks that frightened Angel only served to make Jesse more intriguing to her. "I find him attractive," she confessed. And that was more frightening than anything else about the drifter that she might have admitted.

Their talking woke the baby, but Honey couldn't be sorry because she had been dying for a chance to hold the little boy.

"Aren't you a handsome boy, Rhett,"

Honey cooed as Angel laid the baby in her arms. "Can we take him downstairs?"

Angel seemed hesitant, but Honey urged, "Please?"

"All right." Angel had to face the fact that her fears of Jesse were misplaced in time. She might as well start now.

Dallas and Jesse stopped talking abruptly when the women came downstairs with the baby.

"Look," Honey said, holding Rhett so Jesse could see his face. "Isn't he something?"

Jesse wasn't looking at the child, he was looking at the glow on Honey's face. It was something, all right! She looked radiant and happier than he had ever seen her. He couldn't help imagining how she would look holding their child in her arms.

He frowned, wondering where that idea had come from. He wanted Honey, but babies had a way of tying a man down. Still, he considered the idea and felt things he hadn't anticipated. Pride. Protectiveness. And fear.

Was Honey still young enough to carry a child without any danger to her health? She didn't look over thirty, but he knew she had to be older because Jack was thirteen.

"How old were you when Jack was born?" Jesse asked.

Honey was surprised by the question. "Eighteen. Cale and I married right out of high school."

That made her thirty-two. Three years younger than he was. Maybe the better question was whether he was too old to be a father. He hadn't realized until just now how much he wanted a child of his own someday. Maybe he'd better not put it off too much longer.

"Do you wish you had more children?" he asked Honey.

She never took her eyes off the baby's face. Jesse watched her fingers smooth over the tiny eyebrows, the plump cheeks, the rosy mouth and then touch the tiny fingertips that gripped her little finger. "Oh, yes," she breathed.

She looked up at him and his heart leapt to his throat. Her eyes were liquid with feeling. Suddenly he wanted to be gone from here, to be alone with her.

Honey saw the fierce light in Jesse's eyes but knew she had nothing to fear. The fierceness thrilled her. The light drew her in and warmed her. Jesse Whitelaw was a danger to her, all right. But only because he had the power to steal her heart.

Honey was never sure later how they managed to take their leave so quickly, but she was grateful to be on her way home. In the darkness of the pickup cab she could hug her thoughts to herself. It was only after they had gone several miles that she thought to ask, "Did you tell Dallas about that suspicious man I saw on my property today?"

There was only the slightest hesitation before Jesse replied, "Yes. He said he'd look into it."

"Did you have a good time tonight?"

"I had forgotten how much Dallas and I have in common," he said.

"Oh?" She hadn't thought the two of them were much alike at all. "Like what?"

Jesse was quiet so long Honey didn't think he was going to answer. At last he said, "I can't think of any one thing. Just a feeling I had." He couldn't say more to Honey without raising questions that he wasn't prepared to answer.

"How did you like Angel?"

"Fine." *When she wasn't cringing from me.* He couldn't say that to Honey, either. He wasn't sure what it was about him that frightened Angel Masterson. He only knew she was terrified of him. His lip curled in disgust. She had probably heard stories about the savage Comanche. A hundred years ago his forebears had been savage. Perhaps Angel had been a victim of Comanches in another life.

Jesse shrugged off the uncomfortable feeling he got when he remembered Angel's fear of him. There was something about her that bothered him as much as he bothered her. If he stuck around long enough, maybe someday he would find out what it was.

"Jesse? Is something wrong?"

He hadn't realized he was frowning until Honey spoke. He wiped the expression off his face and said, "No. I'm okay."

"Can I ask you something?"

"Anything."

"Why didn't you tell me you have a family?"

Jesse shrugged. "It didn't seem important."

Family not important? Honey shook her head in despair. Everything she learned about Jesse confirmed him as a loner. She had to stay away from him if she wanted to survive his eventual leave-taking heartwhole.

"Now I want to ask a question," Jesse said.

"What?"

"Why did you marry so young?"

"I was in love." She paused. "And pregnant."

That wasn't the answer he had been expecting, but it didn't really surprise him. He could imagine her youthful passion. He had tasted a little of it himself.

"Were you ever sorry?"

How could she answer that? Maybe she regretted losing some of her choices. But she didn't regret having Jack. As for having to marry . . .

"I met Cale when I was fourteen years old and fell in love with him at first sight," she said. "I never wanted to be anything but Cale's wife, the mother of his children, and to work by his side on the Flying Diamond."

Honey had never put her feelings into words, but it made her loss seem even greater when she realized that her whole life had been focused on Cale. Now that Cale was gone, she was forced to admit that they had never had the partnership she had imagined when she married him. Those youthful dreams were gone. The children were only hers to love for a little while before they grew up and left her. All she would have in the end was the Flying Diamond. Except now the Flying Diamond was being threatened as well.

"I wish someone would catch those rustlers," she said, expressing her fears aloud. "About the only thing that's keeping the ranch afloat with the losses I've had is the service fees I get for General. I sure can't afford to lose any more stock."

He thought of the devastation she would feel when the bull was stolen, but pushed it from his mind. "You won't be losing any more cattle," Jesse said and then could have bitten his tongue.

"How can you be so sure?"

He shrugged. "Just a feeling I have."

One of those uncomfortable silences fell between them. Honey chewed her lower lip, wondering whether she ought to ask a question that had been on her mind lately. She saw the two-story ranch house come into sight and realized she would lose the opportunity to speak if she didn't do it now.

"Were you ever married?" she asked.

Jesse's brow rose at the personal nature of the question. "No."

"Why not?"

His dark eyes glittered in the light from the dashboard as he turned to her and said, "Never found the right woman."

Honey shivered at the intensity of the

look he gave her. On a subconscious level she was aware they had arrived at the house, that he had turned off the car engine, and that this time he had parked the truck in the shadows away from the front porch light.

"Honey?"

His voice rasped over her like a rough caress. She felt his need but wasn't sure what to do. She leaned toward him only a fraction of an inch. It was all the invitation he needed.

Jesse's hand threaded into her hair and tugged her closer. Their mouths were a breath apart but he didn't close the distance.

"Honey?"

He was forcing her to make a choice.

Honey drew back abruptly at a loud tapping on the window.

"Hey, Mom! You guys coming inside or what?" Jack shouted through the glass.

Honey closed her eyes and took a deep breath. Oh Lord. She had forgotten about her overprotective teenage son. He hadn't done anything quite this blatant with Adam, but apparently he recognized Jesse as a greater threat. He wasn't far wrong. She didn't understand the strength of her attraction to the hired hand, but she realized now she would be a fool to underestimate it.

She glanced at Jesse to see how he was handling the interruption and was surprised to see a smile on his face.

"I'm glad you're finding this so amusing," she said.

"If what I suspect is true, Jack hasn't allowed you much privacy with Philips. I have to be eternally grateful to him for that."

"You don't seem too worried that he's going to get in your way."

Jesse grinned. "Nope."

"Why not?"

"Because I don't intend to let him."

Right there, with Jack staring aghast through the window, Jesse took her in his arms and kissed her soundly. Then he reached across her and opened the truck door on her side, gently nudging Jack out of the way.

"Why don't you escort your mom inside, Jack. I've got some things I have to do."

Honey stepped out of the truck without thinking and stood with Jack as Jesse backed the truck and headed down the road that led off Flying Diamond property.

When the truck was gone, Jack confronted his mother in the faint light from the porch.

"Why'd you let him kiss you, Mom?"

"Jack, I —" Honey didn't know what to say.

"You're not gonna marry him or anything, are you?"

That she could answer more easily. "No, I'm not going to marry him." He wasn't going to be around long enough for that.

"Then why'd you kiss him?" Jack persisted.

"I like Jesse a lot, Jack. When two adults like each other, kissing is a way of expressing that feeling. When you're a little older, you'll understand."

"Well, I don't like it," Jack said. "And I don't like him, either."

Honey thought of how hard it was for her son to accept another man in Cale's place, and to share his mother, whom he'd had to himself for the past year. "You know, Jack, just because I kissed another man doesn't mean I'll ever love your father any less. Or you and Jonathan, either."

"Oh, yeah? Well, Dad wouldn't like it."

"Dad would understand," Honey said quietly. "He wouldn't want us to stop living because he's not here with us. You're going to keep growing, Jack, and changing.

Dad wouldn't have wanted you to stay a little boy. He'd want you to grow into the man you're destined to be.

"And I don't think he would necessarily want me to spend the rest of my life alone, without ever loving another man."

Jack jumped on the one word that stuck out in all she'd said. "Are you saying you're in *love* with that drifter?"

"No." *But I could be.*

Honey put her hand on Jack's shoulder, but he shrugged away from her. She ignored the snub as they headed up the porch steps and into the house. "Let's just take each day one at a time, shall we? I hope you'll give Jesse the benefit of the doubt. I don't love him, but I do like him, Jack. I'd appreciate it if you could try to get along with him."

"I'll try," Jack said. "But I'm not promising you anything."

"That's all I can ask," Honey said.

After she had sent Jack to bed, Honey stood at the lace-curtained window in her bedroom and looked out into the dark.

Where are you, Jesse Whitelaw? What brought you here? And what do you want from me?

It was three in the morning before Honey heard the front door open and close. Jesse was back. She sat up, thinking to confront him about where he had been. Then she lay back down.

He wasn't her husband. He wasn't accountable to her. And it was none of her business what he had been doing. Or with whom.

Honey closed her eyes. When Cale died she had made up her mind never to let another man break her heart. She lay on her side and pulled the covers up over her shoulder. She was going to put that drifting man out of her mind once and for all.

Maybe Jack was right. From now on, she would keep a little more distance between herself and the hired hand.

Five

Jesse had known he was heading into deep water the first time he touched Honey Farrell. But it had been impossible to ignore the woman. There was something about her that called to him. He had no business getting involved with anyone, not with the life he led. Yet he hadn't been able to control the desire for her that rocked him whenever she was near. His attraction to her was as strong now, three weeks after he had first laid eyes on her, as it had been that first night. Once having tasted Honey, having touched her, it was an exercise of will to keep his distance from her.

He had been a fool to take that room off the kitchen. He could have found a way to steal General without arousing suspicion even if he were living in the barn. It was rough enough seeing Honey every morning for breakfast, without knowing that he didn't have the right to hold her the way he wanted.

As it turned out, he had ended up seeking out the room in the barn at odd times — like now — for the privacy it offered him. Jesse crossed his arms behind his head and lay back on the bunk. The room offered few amenities. The bed was hard and the walls were unadorned wooden slats. It smelled always of leather and hay. But at least here he could get away from her to think. Right now he had a lot to think about.

Something had happened this morning that he wasn't sure he wanted to remember, but he was quite sure he would never forget.

He had woken at the break of dawn, since he and Honey had agreed that he should have use of the bathroom first each morning. As he climbed the stairs wearing no more than jeans and socks, scratching his bare chest, he distinctly heard the water running. He had wondered what Honey was doing up so early. Over the past three weeks she had kept her bedroom door closed until he had bathed and shaved and headed back downstairs to make coffee. Then she would bathe and join him to finish making breakfast before the boys awoke.

Jesse had been curious enough about the change in routine to continue to the bathroom door. He knocked, but there was no answer.

"Honey?"

When she didn't respond, he tried the door. It wasn't locked, so he cautiously opened it. He wasn't sure what he expected, but what he found was disturbing.

Water was lapping at the edge of the tub, threatening to overflow. Honey was lying back with her nape against the edge of the tub. Her face was angled away from him. Her hair was wet and slicked back to reveal the plane of her jaw. In the steam-fogged room she provided an almost ethereal vision. He stood transfixed, staring at her.

"Honey?"

Concerned when there was still no response he stepped forward and knelt beside the tub. He gasped at his first glorious sight of her naked body. Before desire could take hold, he caught sight of her face, frozen in a mask of agony. Certain that something was seriously wrong, he rose to shut off the water and in the same deft move reached for a towel to wrap around her.

When he lifted her from the water, her eyes remained closed. Her face was frozen in a tragic pose like some marble statue. He picked her up in his arms and, rather than stay in the steamy room, headed for the open door down the hall that led to her bedroom. She offered no resistance, which

101

made him even more concerned. Once inside, he shoved the door closed with his shoulder and carried her over to the canopied bed.

He wondered if her husband had slept with her in this frilly room, but decided she must have redone it since his death. It was a feminine place now, with the lace canopy overhead and lace curtains at the windows. It smelled of some flower, which he finally identified as the same honeysuckle scent he had breathed so often in the bathroom.

He tried to lay her on the bed but she grasped him around the neck, refusing to let go. He sat down on the bed and pulled her farther into his arms.

It was then that he realized she was crying. Sobbing, actually. Only there was no sound, just the heaving of her body and the closed, distorted features on her face.

"It's all right," he crooned. "You're all right. I'm here now."

Her grip tightened around his neck and her nose nuzzled against his throat. She moaned once, and the silent sobbing began again.

Jesse felt his throat swell with emotion. His arms tightened around her, as though he could protect her from whatever was causing her pain. Only he hadn't a clue as to why she was so distraught.

"It's all right, Honey. Nothing can hurt you. I'm here. You're fine."

He meant what he said. He wouldn't allow anyone or anything to harm her. Jesse tightened his arms possessively, only to feel her struggle against his hold. Which reminded him he had no right to feel such feelings. They were virtual strangers. He knew little about her; and she knew nothing, really, about him.

He loosened his hold, caressing her bare shoulders in preparation for moving them apart. As soon as he tried to separate them, she clutched at him and buried her face even deeper against his chest. He was perfectly willing to hold her all day, if that was what she needed. He settled himself more comfortably, putting his stockinged feet on the bedspread, to wait out her tears.

She cried herself to sleep.

Jesse watched the sun rise with a sleeping woman in his arms. He had always wondered what it would be like to settle down, to have a woman of his own, to wake like this with her softness enfolded in his arms. His life hadn't allowed such a luxury. Lately he had begun to wonder whether he ought to think more seriously about finding a wife.

He had bitter experience already with one woman who hadn't been able to handle the kind of life he led. She had worried and begged and cried for him to change his ways. But he hadn't been able — or willing — to give up the life he had planned for himself. It had been a bitter separation, and he had learned that he could hurt, and be hurt.

That had been nearly ten years ago. He hadn't allowed himself to fall in love again. Or to dream about a permanent woman in his life.

Until he had met Honey.

Jesse brushed back a drying wisp of curl from Honey's brow. He had no idea what it was about this woman that made her different from every other. She was like the other half of him; with her he felt whole. He worried about what would happen when she knew the truth about him.

Maybe it wouldn't matter.

Jesse grimaced. It would matter.

At least the boys weren't around this morning. He shuddered to think what Jack would have said if he caught Jesse in Honey's bedroom — no matter how innocent the circumstances. Fortunately, since yesterday had been the last day of school, Jack had gone off to an end-of-school party and stayed the night with friends. Jonathan was spending the first six weeks of summer vacation with Honey's mother and father.

Jesse felt Honey stir in his arms and thought how well the name fit her, for she flowed around him, her softness conforming to all his hard planes. He smoothed the damp hair as best he could. "How are you feeling?"

She stiffened in his arms. "Jesse? What are you doing here?"

"You don't remember?"

She frowned. "No . . . yes . . . oh."

He watched an endearing pink blush begin at her neck and rise to her face as she realized she was naked under the towel. It had slipped some since he had carried her into the room. Now it exposed a rounded hip and teased him with the edge of one honey-brown nipple. He found the sight enchanting.

She tried to ease herself away.

"There's no sense worrying now," he said. "I've already seen everything there is to see. But I would like to hear what had you so upset."

Her shoulders sagged. For a moment he thought she wasn't going to tell him. When she did, he wished she hadn't.

"Yesterday would have been my four-teenth wedding anniversary. I couldn't get Cale out of my mind all night. I guess I was hoping to soak the memories out of my system — the sad ones, anyway."

"Did it work?"

Her face was surprisingly serene when she answered, "I think maybe it did. I feel better anyway. Thanks for being there. I hadn't realized how much I needed . . . someone . . . to hold me."

Once Jesse was reassured that Honey was no longer in pain, it left him free to ac-knowledge the other feelings that arose from holding her in his arms. And to pursue them.

"I wouldn't be honest if I didn't say I'm enjoying this," he said. "You're a beautiful woman, Honey." He felt his body tighten and knew she must feel the swell of arousal beneath her.

Honey tried to sit up, but Jesse kept her where she was. "No need trying to pretend you didn't hear what I said. I've kept my distance the past three weeks, but it hasn't been easy. I want you, Honey. I don't want to fight what I'm feeling anymore."

"How can you say something like that when you know I've spent the night crying over another man?"

"Cale is dead, Honey. You're entitled to your memories of him. But I won't let him come between us."

"There is no *us!*" Honey protested. "You're a drifter, Jesse. Here today and gone tomorrow. I can't —"

His voice was fierce because he feared she was right. "We have today," he said. "I can't offer you a tomorrow right now. Believe me, if I could, I would."

He could see that she wanted him, that she was tempted to take today and say to hell with tomorrow. He wished he could make promises, but a man in his line of work couldn't do that. So he held his tongue, his jaw taut as he waited to hear her answer.

"If it were only me," she began, "I might be willing to accept what you have to offer. But I have two sons. I have to think of them. You're a drifter, Jesse. You could never stay in one place long enough to be the father they need."

"What if I said I could?" She lifted her blue eyes to him and he saw they were filled with hope . . . and despair.

"I'd like to believe you. But I can't."

"So you're posting a No Trespass sign?" he asked.

"I didn't say that."

"Then what are you saying?"

"I have to think about it," she retorted. She looked up into Jesse's dark eyes seeking answers for her confused feelings. His gaze was intent, his lids hooded, his mouth rigid, tense with desire.

Suddenly she was aware again of her half-naked state and of the hard male body beneath her. Jesse put a hand on her bottom and shifted her so she was lying with the heart of her pressed to the heat of him.

She gasped. Honey had forgotten the pleasure of a man's hard body pressed against her softness.

"Ah, sweetheart, that feels so good," Jesse murmured.

She clutched at his shoulders, afraid to move lest she succumb to the pleasure or have to give it up. She closed her eyes and laid her head against his chest. He felt strong, and she felt secure in his arms, as though she could have no more worries if they faced the world together.

He was offering himself for a while. For the moment. Honey realized suddenly that she was seriously considering his offer. She didn't want to fall in love with him. That way lay disaster. When he left he would break her heart. But she couldn't deny that when she was with him she felt safe and, curiously, loved. It was a feeling she'd had with no other man since Cale's death.

She would be a fool to live for today; she would be a fool to give up today for the hope of tomorrow. But maybe the time had come for acting a little foolish. Knowing her decision was made, Honey relaxed and nuzzled her face against Jesse's throat.

He felt her acquiescence. Her body flowed once more like honey, hot and smooth. His blood began to thrum.

Honey suddenly felt herself being rolled over onto her back. Jesse lay on top of her, his hips pressed tightly into the cradle of her thighs, so there was no mistaking his intention. He levered himself onto his palms and she felt herself quivering as he took a long, lazy look at the breasts he had exposed.

"You're so beautiful," he rasped.

He lowered his mouth so slowly that Honey felt the curl of desire in her belly long before his mouth reached the tip of her breast. She anticipated his touch, but the reality was stunning. The warmth. The heat. The wetness of his tongue. The sharp pain as his teeth grazed the crest, and then the strong sucking as he took her breast into his mouth. It was almost more pleasure than she could bear.

Honey was frantic to touch his flesh, and her fingernails made distinct crescents in his back as his mouth captured hers and his tongue ravaged her.

Honey shuddered as his hand cupped her breast. He kneaded the tip between his callused finger and thumb, causing a feeling that was exquisite. There were too many sensations to cope with them all. The roughness of his hands, the wetness of his mouth, the heaviness of his lower body on hers. She was lost in sensation.

With Cale, they would have rushed to fulfillment. But when she reached for the metal buttons of Jesse's fly, his hand was there to stop her. It seemed he had not nearly had his fill of touching and tasting. He held her hand tight against the bulge in his jeans for a moment, then laid her palm against his cheek.

"Touch me, Honey. I need you to touch me."

And she did. Her fingertips roamed his face as though she were a blind woman trying to see him for the first time. She found the tiny scar in his hairline and the spiderweb of lines beside his eyes. The thickness of his brows. The petal softness of his eyelids and his feathery lashes.

She searched out the hollow beneath his cheekbone and the strength of his jaw. The long, straight nose and beneath it the twin lines that led to his lips, soft and damp and full.

He nipped her fingertips and made her laugh until his teeth caught the pad between her fingers and thumb. His love bite chased waves of feeling down her spine.

She used lips and teeth and tongue to trace the shell shape of his ear and was rewarded with a masculine groan that fought its way up through clenched teeth. She was lost in an adventure of discovery, so she wasn't aware, at first, of similar forays Jesse was making.

He nibbled at her neck and laved the love bites with his tongue. Honey felt her whole body clench in response. His hands entwined with hers, and he held them down on either side of her head so she couldn't interfere with his sensual exploration. His lips traced the length of her collarbone and slipped down to the tender skin beneath her arm. He bit and suckled until Honey was bucking beneath him.

"Jesse, please," she begged. She couldn't have said herself whether she wanted him to stop or go on.

Jesse certainly had no intention of stopping. He was fascinated by the woman under him. By her scents and textures and tastes. She smelled of honeysuckle, but her taste was distinct, a woman taste that was meant for him and him alone. Her skin was like satin, or maybe silk, smooth and alluring. He couldn't touch her enough, couldn't taste her enough.

His mouth found hers again, and he brought their bodies into alignment, feeling the moist heat of her through the denim that still separated them. He wanted her. How he wanted her!

He released her hands to reach down toward his Levi's, but her hand was there before him.

"Let me."

Her eyes were lambent, heavy-lidded, the blue almost violet with desire. His loins tightened. He couldn't speak, so he nodded curtly.

She took her own damn sweet time with it. A button at a time he felt himself come free until she was holding him, surrounding him with her hand.

He hissed out a breath. "Damn woman. You're going to kill me with kindness."

Honey smiled seductively. "Then you'll die smiling, cowboy."

The crooked grin flashed on his face and was gone an instant later as she led him toward the female portal that awaited him.

He paused long enough to rasp out, "Are you protected?"

She nodded at the same time he thrust himself inside her. *Hot. Wet. Tight.* The feelings were astounding, and he groaned as he seated himself deep within her body.

For a moment he didn't move, just enjoyed the feeling of being inside her, of having joined the two of them as one. *Right. It felt right. And good.*

"Honey, dammit, I —" He wanted to wait even longer, arouse her more, until she couldn't talk or even breathe. It was soon apparent she was as aroused as he. Her hands shoved his jeans down and she grasped his buttocks as her legs came up around him. He took his weight on his hands, leaving him free to caress her lips and breasts with his mouth.

Jesse felt a frenzy of uncontrollable need for this woman, at this moment in time. "Honey, I can't —"

He needn't have worried that he was leaving her behind. He felt the convulsions deep inside her and knew she had reached the same pinnacle as he. He threw his head back, teeth clenched against the agony of pleasure that swelled through him as he spilled his seed. He was unaware of the exultant cry that escaped him at that ultimate moment.

Honey felt the tears steal into the corners of her eyes as Jesse slipped to her side and pulled her into his arms. She held on to him tightly, afraid to admit the awesomeness of what had just happened between them. It wasn't what she had expected. The pleasure, yes. But the feeling of belonging . . . That, she couldn't explain and didn't want to contemplate.

"Honey? Did I hurt you?"

She felt his lips at the corners of her eyes, kissing away the tears. "No," she said. "You didn't hurt me."

"Then, why — ?"

"I don't know," she admitted in a choked voice. Another tear fell.

He pulled her into his embrace. In a low voice, that rusty-gate voice, he said, "It felt right, Honey. It felt good. Don't be sorry."

"I'm not," she said. And realized she wasn't. Cale was dead; she was alive. She didn't fool herself. What she and Jesse had just experienced was rare. It hadn't even happened all the time with Cale. That must mean that she felt more for the drifter than even she had previously perceived. She wasn't ready yet to examine those feelings. She wasn't sure what she would find. She certainly wasn't ready to confront them head-on.

Honey changed the subject instead. "Jack will be showing up soon," she whispered.

"Yeah. I'd better get out of here." He grinned and slicked his hand through hair damp with sweat. "I could really use a bath."

Honey arched a brow. "Are you bragging or complaining?"

His eyes were suddenly serious as he said, "I got exactly what I wanted. Are you saying you didn't want it, too?"

"No. I'm not saying that."

He searched her eyes, trying to discern her feelings. First and foremost among them was confusion. Well, he could identify with that. Perhaps what they both needed now was time and distance. Especially since he could feel himself becoming aroused again simply by her nearness. "I'd better get that bath."

He pulled his Levi's back on and buttoned them partway, knowing he was just going to pull them off again down the hall, then turned back to look at Honey.

She had grabbed the towel and was

using it to cover herself.

"I think I find you even more enticing half-clothed than when you're naked," he warned.

Honey clutched the towel closer, accidentally revealing even more skin. She was helpless to resist him if he touched her again.

Jesse considered making love to her again, but his common sense stopped him. Any moment Jack might return home. While he hadn't allowed her son's objections to prevent him from pursuing Honey, he didn't want to confront Jack coming from her bedroom, either. He didn't want the boy thinking any less of his mother because of her relationship with some drifter. When the time was right, he would tell them all the truth and let Honey decide whether she wanted anything more to do with him — or not.

He finished his bath and went downstairs to make coffee, as usual. Shortly thereafter he was joined by Honey, fresh from her bath and looking even more alluring with her hair curling in damp tendrils around her face. She was wearing the same man's robe she had worn the first day he had arrived. He wondered if she had done it on purpose, to remind him that she had belonged to another man. He wanted to cross the room and pull her into his arms, but the wary look on her face held him apart.

"I started coffee," he said, to break the uncertain silence.

"How about eggs and bacon this morning?" she asked, heading for the refrigerator.

He let her pass by him without reaching out, but his nostrils flared as he caught the scent of honeysuckle from her hair. He watched her do all the normal things she had done for the past three weeks, as though nothing momentous had happened between them in the bed upstairs.

Then he saw her hands were trembling and realized she wasn't as calm as she wanted him to believe. He didn't think, just closed the distance between them. He had put his hands on her shoulders when a noise behind him froze them both.

"Hey, what's going on here?" Jack said belligerently, shoving open the kitchen door and letting himself in.

Jesse turned to face Honey's older son, but he didn't take his hands from her shoulders. "Your mom's making breakfast."

"That's not what I mean and you know it," Jack retorted.

Jesse saw the tension in the boy's shoulders, the suspicion in his eyes. There was no purpose to be served by aggravating him. He let go of Honey's shoulders, picked up the pot of coffee from the stove and returned to the table to pour himself a cup.

Jack watched with hostile eyes from the doorway, then marched over to stand before the hired hand.

Jessie had been expecting Jack to confront him, but he wasn't prepared for the bluntness of the boy's attack.

"You stay away from my mother. She doesn't want anything to do with you."

"That's her decision, isn't it?"

"I can take care of things around here now that school's out!" the boy said. "We don't need you."

Jesse heard the pain beneath the defiant words. "From what I've seen, your mother can use another helping hand."

"You can never replace my father!" Jack said. "He was a Texas Ranger, a hero. You're nothing, just some drifter who rolled in like tumbleweed. Why don't you go back where you came from?"

"Jack!" Honey was appalled at Jack's attack on Jesse. "Apologize," she ordered.

"I won't!" Jack said. "I meant every word I said. We don't need him here."

"But we do need him," Honey contradicted. "I can't do it all, Jack. Even though you're a big help, there are jobs you can't do, either. We need a man's help. That's why Jesse is here."

Honey realized immediately that she had used the wrong appeal with her son. He was a youth on the verge of manhood, and she had reminded him that despite the change in his voice and his tall lanky body, he was not yet a man.

"Fine!" he retorted. "Keep your hired hand. But don't expect me to like it!"

With that he shoved his way out the screen door and headed for the barn. Without breakfast. Which, knowing Jack's appetite, gave Honey some idea just how upset he was.

Honey felt the tears glaze her eyes. "I'm sorry that happened."

Jesse put his hands on her shoulders to comfort her. "He'll be all right."

"I wish I could be as sure of that as you seem to be."

"Don't worry, Honey. Everything will work out fine. You'll see."

But as he lay in the bunk in the barn, he felt a knot in his stomach at all the hurdles that would have to be crossed if he was ever to claim this woman as his own.

Six

Jesse found Jack in the barn brushing General. He stuck a boot on the bottom rail of the stall door and leaned his forearms on the top rail.

"You and that bull seem to be good friends," Jesse said.

The boy ignored him and continued brushing the bull's curly red coat.

Jesse tipped his hat back off his brow. "When I was a kid about your age my dad gave me a bull of my very own to raise."

"I was eight when Dad bought General," Jack said. "He wasn't much to look at then, but Dad thought he was something pretty special. He was right. General's always been a winner." Jack seemed embarrassed at having said so much and began brushing a little harder and faster.

"Sounds like your dad was something pretty special, too," Jesse said.

"You're nothing like him, that's for sure!"

"No, I expect not," Jesse agreed. "I do have one thing in common with your father."

Jesse waited for the boy's curiosity to force him to continue the conversation.

"What's that?" Jack asked.

"Feelings for your mother."

Jack glared at him. "Why can't you just leave her alone?"

How could he explain what he felt for Honey in words the boy would understand? Jesse wondered. What did one say to a thirteen-year-old boy to describe the relationship between a man and a woman? It would be easier if he could tell the boy he was committed in some way to Honey. But Jesse had never spoken of "forever" with Honey, and he wasn't free to do so until his business here was done.

"I wish I had an easy answer for your question," Jesse said quietly. "But I don't. Will it help if I say I'll try my damnedest never to do anything that'll hurt your mom?"

Abruptly Jack stopped brushing the bull. "She's never gonna love you like she loved Dad. You're crazy if you think she will. There's no sense in you hanging around. Now that school's out, I can handle things. Why don't you just leave?"

"I can't," Jesse said simply.

"Why not?"

"Your mother needs my help." *And I still*

have to steal this bull.

Jack's body sagged like a balloon losing air. "I wish Dad was still alive," he said in a quiet, solemn voice.

Jesse retrieved a piece of hay from the feed trough and began to shred it. "My father died when I was twenty," he said. "Bronc threw him and broke his neck. I didn't think anything could hurt so much as the grief I felt losing him. I missed him so much, I left home and started wandering. It took a few years before I realized he was still with me."

The boy's brow furrowed, revealing the confusion caused by Jesse's last statement.

Jesse reached out to scratch behind the huge bull's ears. "What I mean is, I'd catch myself doing something and remember how my dad had been the one to teach it to me. My father left me with the best part of himself — the memories I have of everything he said and did."

Jack swallowed hard. His teeth gritted to stop the tremor in his chin.

"Your mom won't ever forget your dad, Jack. No more than you will. No matter who comes into her life, she'll always have her memories of him. And so will you."

Jesse wasn't sure whether his words had caused any change in Jack's attitude toward him, but he didn't know what else to say.

The silence deepened and thickened until finally Jesse said, "You're doing a fine job grooming General, boy. When you get done, I could use some help replacing a few rotted posts around the corral."

Jesse turned and left the barn without waiting for a reply from Jack. Fifteen minutes later, Jack appeared at his side wearing work gloves and carrying a shovel. The two of them labored side by side digging out several rotten posts and replacing them with new ones.

Honey could hardly believe her eyes when she looked out the kitchen window. She forced herself to remain inside and give Jesse and Jack time alone together. When several hours had passed and they were still hard at work, she prepared a tray with two large glasses of iced tea and took it out to the corral.

"You both look thirsty," she said.

Jesse swiped at the dripping sweat on his neck and chest with a bandanna he had pulled from his back pocket. "I am. How about you, Jack?"

Honey was amazed at the even, almost cordial sound of her son's voice as he said, "I feel dry enough to swallow a river and come back for more."

Both males made short work of the tall glasses of iced tea. Honey flushed when Jesse winked at her as he set his glass back on the tray. She looked quickly at Jack to see how he reacted to Jesse's flirtatious behavior. Her son shrugged . . . and grinned!

She turned and stared in amazement at Jesse. What on earth had he said to Jack to cause such a miraculous reversal in her son's attitude? Honey frowned as the two shared a look of male understanding. Whatever it was, she ought to feel grateful. And she did. Sort of.

Honey tried to pinpoint what it was that bothered her about Jack's acceptance of the drifter. Her forehead wrinkled in thought as she slowly made her way back to the house. She wasn't pleased with the conclusions she reached.

So long as Jack found the drifter a threat and an interloper, it had been easier for Honey to justify keeping Jesse at an emotional arm's length. She had realized there was no sense letting herself get attached to him if one of her children clearly abhorred him. Jack's sudden acceptance of Jesse left her without a piece of armor she had counted on. Now, with her defenses down, she was extremely vulnerable to the drifter's entreaties.

Halfway to the house, the phone started ringing. Honey was breathless from running when she finally answered it. "Honey? Did I catch you outside again?"

"Oh, Adam. Uh, yes, you did. When are you coming home?"

"I am home. Are you free to go out tonight?"

Honey thought about it for a moment. Clearly she needed to be sure Jesse wasn't anywhere around when she told Adam she couldn't marry him. Going out was probably not a bad idea. "Sure," she said at last. "What time should I meet you and where?"

"I'll pick you up."

"That isn't necessary, Adam. I —"

"I insist."

It was clear he wouldn't take no for an answer. Rather than argue, she agreed. "All right."

"See you at eight, Honey."

Honey almost groaned aloud at Adam's purring tone of voice when he said her name. It was not going to be a pleasant evening. "At eight," she confirmed.

When Jesse and Jack came into the house for supper they found only two places set at the table. It was the most subtle way Honey could think of to say that she was going out for the evening. From the look in Jesse's eyes, subtlety wasn't going to help much.

It was Jack who asked, "Aren't you going to eat with us?"

"No. Adam is taking me out to supper."

Identical frowns settled on two male faces. It had apparently dawned on Jack that his mother had not one, but two suitors. Honey would have laughed at the chagrined expression on her son's face if the situation hadn't been so fraught with tension.

Jack looked warily at Jesse. "Uh . . . Adam is mom's . . . uh . . . friend," he said by way of explanation.

"That's what your mom said," Jesse agreed.

Jack relaxed when it appeared Jesse wasn't upset by the situation. He turned to his mother and asked, "Are you going to tell Adam tonight that you won't marry him?"

Honey clutched her hands together, frustrated by the situation Jack had put her in. The gleam of amusement in Jesse's dark eyes didn't help matters any. She simply said, "Adam deserves an answer to his pro- posal. And yes, I intend to give it to him tonight."

"And?" Jack prompted.

"After I've given Adam my answer, I'll be glad to share it with you," she said to Jack. "Until then, I think you should sit down and eat your supper."

Honey escaped upstairs to dress, where she managed to consume most of the two hours until Adam's expected arrival at eight.

Shortly before Adam was due to arrive, Jack knocked on her door and asked if he could spend the night with a friend.

"What time will you be home tomorrow morning?" Honey asked.

"Well, me and Reno were thinking maybe we'd go tubing tomorrow. I figured I'd stay and have lunch with him and spend the afternoon on the river."

"Jack, I don't think —"

"It's the first Saturday of summer vacation, Mom! You aren't gonna make me come home and work, are you?"

Jack knew exactly what to say to push her maternal guilt buttons. "All right," she relented. "But I don't think you can make a habit of this. I'm depending on your help around the ranch this summer."

"Believe me, Mom, it's just this once."

Moments later Jack came by with his overnight bag thrown over his shoulder to give her a quick, hard hug. Then he scampered down the stairs and out through the kitchen. She heard the screen door slam behind him.

If Honey thought she had managed to avoid a confrontation with Jesse by staying in her room until the very last minute, she was disabused of that notion as soon as she descended the stairs. He was waiting for her at the bottom.

"You told me you aren't going to marry that Philips guy," Jesse said.

Honey postponed any response by heading for the living room. She brushed aside the lacy drapery on the front window and looked for the headlights of Adam's sports car in the distance. No rescue there. She turned and faced Jesse, who had followed her into the room and was standing behind the aged leather chair that had been Cale's favorite spot in the room.

"I've never given Adam an answer to his proposal," Honey said. "He deserves to be told my decision face-to-face."

"Tell him here. Don't go out with him."

Honey felt a surge of anger. "I may not be willing to marry Adam, but I care for him as a person. I agreed to go to dinner with him, and I'm going!"

She watched Jesse's eyes narrow, his nostrils flare, his lips flatten. His anger clearly matched her own. But he didn't argue further.

Neither did he leave the room. When Adam arrived five long minutes later, he found Jesse comfortably ensconced in Cale's favorite chair idly perusing a ranching magazine.

Jesse looked up assessingly when Adam entered the living room, but he didn't rise to greet the other man. He kept his left ankle hooked securely over his right knee and slouched a little more deeply into the chair, concentrating on the magazine.

"Don't be too late," he said as Adam slipped an arm around Honey to escort her out the door. Jesse smiled behind the magazine when the other man stiffened.

His smugness disappeared when Honey replied with a beatific smile, "Don't wait up for me."

Jesse would have been downright concerned if he could have heard what passed between Honey and Adam in the car on the way to the restaurant.

"That hired hand sure made himself at home in your living room," Adam complained before too many minutes had passed.

Honey sighed in exasperation. "It wasn't what it looked like."

"Oh?"

"He was trying to make you feel uncomfortable," Honey said.

"He succeeded. I wouldn't have been half as upset if it weren't for the things I know about him."

"You've only seen him twice!" Honey protested. "You don't know anything about him."

"Actually, I did some checking up on him."

"Adam, that really wasn't necessary." Honey didn't bother to keep the irritation out of her voice. Men! Really!

"Maybe you'll change your mind when you hear what I have to say."

Honey arched a brow and waited.

"Did you know he's got a criminal record?"

"What? *Jesse?*" Honey felt breathless, as though someone had landed on her chest with both feet. "Dallas vouched for him."

"Dallas obviously covered for his friend. The man's been arrested, Honey." He paused significantly and added, "For rustling cattle."

Honey leapt on the only scrap of positive information Adam had given her. "*Ar-*

rested. Then he was never convicted?"

Adam released a gusty breath. "Not as far as I could find out. Probably had a good lawyer. It was only by chance that there was any record of the arrest. Don't you see, Honey? He might even be one of the rustlers who've been stealing your stock. He probably moved in so he could look things over up close."

"I lost stock long before Jesse showed up around here," Honey said coldly. "I refuse to believe he's part of any gang of rustlers."

But she couldn't help thinking about the night Jesse had been gone until three in the morning. Where had he been? What had he been doing? And Jesse hadn't wanted her to call the police when she had spotted someone suspicious on her property. He had said he would rather tell Dallas about it. Had he?

Adam had given her a lot to think about, and Honey was quiet for the rest of the journey to the restaurant in Hondo. Hermannson's Steak House was famous for its traditional Texas fare of chicken-fried steak and onion rings. A country band played later in the evening, and she and Adam danced the Texas two-step and the rousing and bawdy Cotton-eyed Joe.

Adam was always good company, and

Honey couldn't help laughing at his anec-
dotes. But she was increasingly aware that
the end of the evening was coming, when
Adam would renew his proposal and she
would have to give him her answer. She felt
a somberness stealing over her. Finally
Adam ceased trying to make her smile.

"Time to go?" he asked.

"I think so."

She tried several times in the car to get
out the words *I can't marry you*. It wasn't
as easy being candid as she wished it was.

Adam wasn't totally insensitive to her
plight, she discovered. In fact he made it
easy for her.

"It's all right," he said in a quiet voice. "I
guess I knew I was fooling myself. When
you didn't say yes right away I figured you
had some reservations about marrying me.
I guess I hoped if I was persistent you'd
change your mind."

"I'm sorry," Honey said.

"So am I," Adam said with a wry twist of
his mouth. "I suppose it won't do any good
to warn you again about that drifter you
hired, either."

"I'll think about what you said," Honey
conceded. She just couldn't believe Jesse
had come to the Flying Diamond to steal
from her. She had to believe that or die

from the pain she felt at the thought he had simply been using her all this time.

The inside of the house was dark when they drove up, but it was late. Honey was grateful that she wouldn't have to confront Jesse tonight about the things Adam had told her.

"Good night, Adam," Honey said. She felt awkward. Unsure whether he would want to kiss her and not willing to hurt him any more than she already had by refusing if he did.

Adam proved more of a gentleman than she had hoped. He took her hand in his and held it a moment. The look on his face was controlled, but she saw the pain in his eyes as he said, "Goodbye, Honey."

She swallowed over the lump in her throat. She hadn't meant to hurt him. "I'm sorry," she said again.

"Don't be. I'll survive." Only he knew how deeply he had allowed himself to fall in love with her, and how hard it was to give up all hope of having her for his wife.

Slowly he let her hand slip through his fingers. He came around and opened the car door for her and walked her to the porch. As he left her, his last words were, "Be careful, Honey. Don't trust that drifter too much."

Then he was gone.

Honey let herself into the dark house and leaned back against the front door. Her whole body sagged in relief. She had hurt a good man without meaning to, though she didn't regret refusing his proposal.

"You were gone long enough!"

The accusation coming out of the dark startled Honey and she nearly jumped out of her shoes.

"You scared me to death!" she hissed. "What are you doing sitting here in the dark?"

"Waiting for you."

As her eyes adjusted to the scant light, she saw that Jesse was no longer sitting. He had risen and was closing the distance between them. Escape seemed like a good idea and she started for the stairs. She didn't get two steps before he grasped her by the shoulders.

"You didn't bring him inside with you. Does that mean you've told him things are over between you?"

"That's none of your —"

Jesse shook her hard. "Answer me!"

Honey was more furious than she could remember being at any time since Cale's death. How dare this man confront her!

How dare he demand answers that were none of his business! "Yes!" she hissed. "Yes! Is that what you wanted to hear?"

Jesse answered her by capturing her mouth with his. It was a savage kiss, a kiss of claiming. His hands slid around her and he spread his legs and pulled her into the cradle of his thighs. He wasn't gentle, but Honey responded to the urgency she felt in everything he did. Against all reason, she felt a spark of passion ignite, and she began to return his fervent kisses.

"Honey, Honey," he murmured against her lips. "I need you. I want you."

Honey was nearly insensate with the feelings he was creating with his mouth and hands. He made her feel like a woman with his desire, his need. She shoved at his shoulders and whispered, "Jesse, we can't. Jack is —"

"Jack's spending the night with friends," he reminded her.

He grinned at the stunned look on her face as she realized that her youthful chaperon was not going to come to her rescue this time.

Without giving her a chance to object, Jesse swept her into his arms in a masterful imitation of Rhett and Scarlett and headed upstairs.

"What do you think you're doing?" Honey demanded.

"Taking you to bed where you belong," Jesse said.

"We can't do this," Honey protested.

Jesse stopped halfway up the stairs. "Why not?"

There was a long pause while Honey debated whether to confront him with the accusations Adam had made. "Because . . . You'd never lie to me, would you, Jesse?"

It was dark so she couldn't see his face, but being held in his arms the way she was, she felt the sudden tension in his body.

"I'd never do anything to hurt you, Honey."

"That isn't exactly the same thing, is it?"

There was enough light to see his smile appear. "That's one of the things I like about you, Honey. You don't pull any punches."

"I think you'd better put me down, Jesse," she said.

Slowly he released her legs so her body slid down across his. She was grateful for the way he held on to her, because her feet weren't quite steady under her. Her nipples puckered as he slowly rubbed their bodies together.

"You want me, Honey," he said in his rusty-gate voice.

"It would be hard to deny it without sounding like a fool," she said acerbically.

His mouth found the juncture between her neck and shoulder and blessed it with tantalizing kisses. Honey gripped his arms to keep from falling down the stairs as his mouth sought out the tender skin at her throat and followed it up to her ear. Her head fell back of its own volition, offering him better access. Her whole body quivered at the sensations he was evoking with mouth and teeth and tongue.

A hoarse, guttural sound forced its way past Honey's lips. "Jesse, please."

"What, Honey? What do you want?"

Honey groaned again, and it was as much a sound of pleasure as of despair. "You," she admitted in a harsh voice. "I want you."

Jesse lifted her into his arms and carried her the rest of the way upstairs.

Seven

Honey felt the heat of the man beside her and reached out to caress the muscular strength of a body she now knew as well as her own. When Jesse stirred, Honey withdrew her hand. She didn't want to awaken him. Last night had been magical. She didn't wish to rouse from the night's dream and face the reality of day.

Jesse looked younger in the soft dawn light, though still something of a rogue with the stubble of dark beard that shadowed his face. She rubbed her cheek against the pillow, noticing that her skin was tender where his beard had rubbed again — and again. As were her breasts, she realized with chagrin.

He hadn't been gentle, but then, neither had she. Their lovemaking had blazed with the feelings of desperation that had followed them upstairs to the bedroom.

Honey understood her own reasons for feeling that she had to reach for whatever memories she could make with Jesse before he was gone. She had no idea why Jesse had seemed equally desperate. Had he already made up his mind to leave her? Did he already know the day when their brief interlude would come to an end?

She touched her lower lip, which was tender from the kissing they had done, the love bites he had given her. She must have bitten him, as well. There was a purplish bruise on Jesse's neck, put there in a moment of passion, she supposed. She didn't remember doing it, and she was embarrassed to think what he was going to say when he saw it. She hadn't left such a mark on a man since she'd been a teenager, playing games with Cale.

Honey winced. She hadn't thought of Cale once last night. Jesse hadn't left room for thought. He had spread her legs and thrust inside her, claiming her like some warrior with the spoils of battle. And what had she done? She had allowed it. No, that wasn't precisely true. She had *reveled* in his domination of her. She had opened herself to Jesse and allowed him liberties that Cale had never enjoyed.

And she wasn't even sorry.

Honey had never needed a man so much, or felt so much with a man. She didn't understand it. What made Jesse so different from Adam? Why couldn't she have chosen a man who would give her the security she needed in her life? Why did she have to love —

Honey stopped her thoughts in midstream, appalled by the word that had come to mind. *Love.* Was that why the lovemaking had been so thrilling? Was she in love with Jesse Whitelaw?

It was unfair to be forced to evaluate her feelings when she was staring at the object of her desire. Because she loved the way Jesse's raven-black hair fell across his brow. She loved the way his dark lashes feathered onto bronze cheeks. She loved his mouth, with the narrow upper lip and the full lower one, that had brought her so much pleasure.

She loved the weight of his body on hers when they were caressing each other. She loved the feel of his skin, soft to the touch, and yet hard with corded muscle. She loved the way his flesh heated hers as his callused fingertips sought out her breasts and slid down her belly to the cleft between her thighs.

She loved the feel of their two bodies when they were joined together as a man and woman were meant to be. She loved his patience as he brought her to fulfillment. She loved the lazy-lidded satisfaction in his eyes when she cried out her

pleasure. And she loved the agonized pleasure on his face as he followed her to the
pinnacle of desire they had sought together.

Honey refused to contemplate the other
facets of Jesse's character that appealed to
her. They were many and varied. It was
painful enough to know that she loved him
this way. Because where there was love,
there was hope. And Honey was afraid to
hope that the drifter would be there in the
days to come. She wasn't sure her memories would be enough when he was gone.

Honey knew she couldn't stay in bed any
longer without turning to Jesse yet again.
Rather than be thought a wanton, she
slipped quietly from beneath the covers,
grabbed a shirt, jeans, socks and boots and
headed downstairs to dress in the kitchen.

She didn't make coffee, certain the smell
would wake Jesse, and wanting more time
alone. Honey headed outside to feed the
stock. Maybe she could subdue her unruly
libido with hard work. She entered the
barn and was immediately assailed with familiar smells that comforted and calmed
her. She headed for General's stall and
stopped dead at the sight that greeted her.
Or rather, didn't greet her.

At first Honey refused to believe her

eyes. She gripped the stall where General was supposed to be with white-knuckled hands. Had she left General outside in the corral all night? She was appalled at her thoughtlessness.

Honey ran back outside, but the bull was nowhere to be seen. She hurried back to examine the stall, thinking he might have broken the latch. But it was still hooked.

Staring didn't make the bull appear. He was gone. *Stolen!*

Honey felt despair, followed by rage at the one suspect for the theft who was still within her reach. Purely by instinct, she grabbed two items from the barn as she raced back to the house. She made a brief stop in the kitchen before marching determinedly up the stairs.

Jesse came roaring to life, drenched by the bucket of icy water Honey had thrown on him. "What the hell are you doing, woman?"

He leapt out of bed like a lion from its den, roaring with anger. He was naked, and she had never seen him look so powerful. Or so seductive to her senses.

He grabbed for her and she stepped out of his way. "You bastard!" she hissed.

"Honey, what the hell —"

"Don't come any closer." She held up the buggy whip she had found in the barn, a relic of days gone by. "I'll use this," she threatened.

"What's going on here?" Jesse demanded. "It's a little late for outraged virtue."

"Outraged virtue! You low-down mealy-mouthed skunk!" she raged. "You stole my bull!"

She wanted him to deny it. With all her heart she yearned for him to say he was innocent. But the dark flush she could plainly see working its way up his naked flesh from his powerful shoulders, to his love-bruised neck, landing finally on his strong cheekbones, was as blatant a statement of guilt as she had ever heard.

"How could you?" she breathed, more hurt now than angry. "I trusted you." Then the anger was back, and she wielded the whip with all the fury of humiliation and pain she felt at his betrayal. "I trusted you!"

The whip landed once across his shoulders before he reached out and jerked it from her hands. He threw it across the room and pulled her into his arms.

Honey fought him, beating at him with her fists and kicking at him with her feet until he threw her down on the soaking-wet bed where he subdued her with his weight.

"Stop it, Honey! That's enough!"

"I hate you!" she cried. "I hate you! I hate you!"

She burst into gasping sobs and turned her head away so he wouldn't see the tears she cried over him. She lay still, emotionally devastated, as he kissed them away.

"Honey." His voice sounded like gravel. "I'm sorry."

"Where's — my — bull?" she gritted out between clenched teeth.

"In a safe place," he said.

Honey moaned. His words were final confirmation that he had used her, lied to her, stolen from her.

"It's not what you think," he began.

She turned to face him, eyes blazing. "Can you deny that you lied to me?"

"No, but —

"That you stole General?"

"I did, but —"

She growled deep in her throat and bucked against him.

"If you know what's good for you, you'll lie still," Jesse warned.

Honey froze, suddenly aware of the fact he was naked, and they were in bed.

"Don't you dare touch me. I'll fight you. I'll kick and scratch and —"

"If you'll just shut up for a minute, I can explain everything."

"I don't want to hear your excuses, you bastard. I —"

He kissed her to shut her up.

Honey felt the punishment in his kiss, and it was easy to fight his anger with her own, to arch her body against the weight of his, to grip the male fingers threaded through her own and struggle against his domination.

The more she fought, the more her body responded to the provocation of his. He insinuated his thigh between her legs knowing it would excite her. At the same time his mouth gentled and his lips and tongue came seeking the taste of her, dark like honey, rich and full. She fought his strength, but his hands held hers captive on either side of her head while he ravished her.

"Don't," she pleaded, aware she was succumbing to the desire that had never been far below the surface. "Don't."

She was helpless to deny him. He was stronger than she. To her surprise, he stopped kissing her and raised himself on his elbows so he could look at her.

"Are you ready to listen now?"

She turned her head away and closed her eyes.

He shoved one of her hands back behind her and held it there with the weight of his body while he grabbed her chin with his now-free hand and forced her to look at him.

"Open your eyes and look at me," he commanded.

When she didn't, his mouth came down hard on hers. "Open your eyes, Honey. I'm going to keep kissing you until you do."

Faced with that threat, her eyes flashed open and she glared at him.

His dark eyes burned with fury. His mouth was taut. A muscle jerked in his cheek. "There is an explanation for everything," he gritted out.

"I'll bet!" she retorted.

"Shut up and listen!"

She snorted. But she stayed mute.

He opened his mouth and closed it several times. *Searching for more lies,* Honey thought. He closed his eyes and when he opened them again, she saw regret.

"I don't know how to say this except to say it," he began.

She waited, wondering how she could bear to hear that the man she had spent the night making love to, the man she had begun to think herself in love with, was part of a gang of murdering rustlers.

He took a deep breath and said, "I'm a Texas Ranger. I'm working undercover to catch the leader of the gang of rustlers that's been stealing from ranches in this area."

Honey couldn't believe her ears. Her first reaction was relief. *Jesse wasn't a thief!* The very next was anger — make that fury. *He had lied to her!* It was a lie of omission, but a lie all the same to keep her ignorant of his true identity. Finally there was hopelessness. Which was foolish because she had never really had much hope that the drifter would settle down. Now that she knew Jesse was a Texas Ranger, the situation was clear. *He would leave her when his job was done.* Not that it really mattered. She would never repeat the mistake she had made with Cale.

"Honey? Say something?"

"Let me up."

"Not until I explain."

"You've said enough."

"I didn't want to lie to you, but Dallas —"

"Dallas was in on this? I'll kill him," Honey muttered.

Jesse was pleased by the fire in her eyes

after the awful dullness he had seen when he had told her the truth. Or at least as much of the truth as he could tell her.

"Dallas was under orders, too," Jesse continued. "The Captain thought it would be better if you were kept in the dark. Because of . . ." His voice trailed off as he realized he couldn't tell her the rest of it. "I mean . . . I guess he thought you would understand, having been the wife of a Texas Ranger, why it was necessary."

"I understand, all right," Honey said heatedly. "You used me without a thought to the pain and anguish it would cause."

"How much of what you're feeling is the result of losing General and how much the result of my deceiving you?" Jesse asked in a quiet voice. "General would have been returned within a day or so at the most and no harm done. I hadn't counted on what happened between us, Honey."

"You never should have touched me."

"I know," he said.

"You should have left me completely alone."

"I know," he said.

"Why didn't you?"

"Because I couldn't. I didn't know I would find the other half of myself here, now, under these circumstances."

Honey swallowed over the lump that had suddenly risen in her throat. She closed her eyes to shut out the tenderness in his dark-eyed gaze.

"I love you, Honey."

When her eyes opened they revealed an agony she hadn't ever wanted to feel again. "Don't! Don't say things you don't mean!"

"I've never meant anything more in my life."

"Well, I don't love you!" she retorted.

"Who's lying now, Honey?"

"This can never work, Jesse. Even if you could settle down, and I'm not sure you can, you're a Texas Ranger."

"What does that have to do with anything?"

"I don't want to spend my life worrying about whether you're going to come home to me at the end of the day. I had no choice with Cale. But I have one now. And I choose not to live my life like that."

"I can't — won't — change my life for you," Jesse said, disturbed by the narrow lines she was drawing.

"I'm not asking you to," Honey said.

"Where does that leave us?"

"You've got a job to finish. I assume you're going to meet with the rustlers and exchange General for a great deal of money?"

He grinned crookedly. "That was the plan."

"Then I suggest you go to work."

Jesse sobered for a moment. "Things aren't over between us."

She didn't argue with him. There was no sense in it. As soon as his job was done he would be leaving. She felt the pain of loss already. Even if he had been the drifter he first professed to be, he would have been moving on sooner or later. She had always known Jesse wouldn't be hanging around. Only now his leaving had a certainty that allowed her to begin accepting — and grieving — his loss.

She searched his features, absorbing them, cataloguing them so she would remember them. Her eyes skipped to the body she had adored last night, and she noticed a huge red welt on his right shoulder that had previously been hidden by the pillow.

"Oh, my God, Jesse. Look what I've done to you!"

Jesse gasped as she reached out and touched the spot where the horsewhip had cut into his flesh.

She pushed at his chest. "Let me up, Jesse. I need to get some salve for that before it gets any worse than it is."

Honey didn't know what she would have done if he hadn't let her up just then. She was feeling so many things — remorse and embarrassment and love. And the love seemed to be winning out. She didn't want to care for this man. It would only hurt worse when he left.

Jesse took advantage of the time Honey was out of the room to put on his pants and boots. When she came back he was sitting on the edge of the bed shirtless, waiting for her.

Honey laid the things she had brought back with her on the end table beside the bed, then sat down beside Jesse to minister to the wound.

He hissed in a breath of air when she began dabbing at the raw flesh with warm water. "I know this must hurt," she soothed.

As she worked, Jesse wasn't nearly so aware of the pain as he was of the care she was taking of him. It had been years and years since there had been a woman in his life to care for him. His mother had died when his sister, Tate, was born, leaving Tate to be raised by a father and three older brothers. He had been how old? No more than eleven or twelve.

He luxuriated in the concern Honey

showed with every gesture, every touch. She cared for him. He felt sure of it. Even though she denied him in words, her gentleness, her obvious distress over his injury, gave her away. He meant to have her — despite the reservations she had voiced.

It had never occurred to him that she would demand that he leave the Rangers. He relished the danger and excitement of the job. There must be a way he could have Honey and the Texas Rangers, too. He would just have to find it.

"When are you going to meet with the rustlers?" Honey asked.

"Sometime tonight."

Honey bit her lip to keep from begging him not to go. She had learned her lessons with Cale. Her pleas would be useless. Instead she said, "Promise me you'll be careful."

He took her hand from his shoulder and held it between both of his. "Don't worry about me, Honey." He flashed her a grin. "I've been doing this a long time. I know how to take care of myself. Besides, I'm not about to get myself killed when I've got you to come back to."

"Jesse . . ."

He reached up and caught her chin in

his fingertips, drawing her lips toward his. "Honey . . ."

Warm. Wet. Tender. His mouth seduced her to his will. His hand curled around her nape and slid up into her hair. Suddenly she was sitting in his lap, her hands circling his neck, and his mouth was nuzzling her throat.

"I can't get enough of you," he murmured. "Come back to bed with me, Honey."

She was tempted. Lord how she was tempted!

"Forget about General. Forget about the Texas Rangers. Don't think about —"

Honey tore herself from his grasp and stood facing him. Her breasts ached. Desire spiraled in her belly. It was hard to catch her breath. But catch it she did long enough to say, "No, Jesse. This has to stop. Right now. You can stay here long enough to finish your business. Until then . . . just leave me alone."

Jesse was equally aroused and frustrated by the interruption of their lovemaking. "You're being foolish, Honey."

"So now I'm a fool on top of everything else," she retorted. "You're making it very easy to get you out of my life, Jesse."

He thrust a hand through his hair, making it stand on end. "That came out wrong," he admitted. "You know what I mean."

He rose and paced the floor like a caged wolf. "We're meant to be together. I feel it *here*." He pounded his chest around the region of his heart. "You're only fighting against the inevitable. We *will* spend our lives together."

"Until you get shot?" she retorted. "Until I bury you like I buried Cale? No, Jesse. We aren't going to be together. I need someone I can rely on to be around for the long haul. You aren't that man."

"That remains to be seen," he said through clenched teeth.

Jesse wasn't prepared for the tears that gathered in Honey's eyes. He watched her blink hard, valiantly fighting them. It was clearly a losing battle, and they spilled from the corners of her eyes.

"It's over, Jesse. I mean it." She dashed at the tears with the back of her hand. "*I won't cry for you.*"

He watched her eyes begin to blaze with anger as she battled against the strong emotions that gripped her — and won. The tears stopped, and only the damp streaks on her face remained to show the pain she was suffering.

He felt her retreating from him even

though she hadn't moved a step. "Don't go, Honey. I need you." He paused and added, "I love you."

"You lied to me. You used me. That's not the way people in love treat each other." She choked back the tears that threatened again and said, "You should have told me the truth. You should have trusted me. You should have given me the choice of knowing who you really are before I got involved with you. That's what I can't forgive, Jesse."

She turned and left the room, shoulders back, chin high, proud and unassailable. He had never wanted her more than he did in that moment, when he feared she was lost to him.

He sank down onto the bed and stared out through the lace-curtained window. He had to admit his excuse for keeping Honey in the dark about why he had come to the Flying Diamond had sounded feeble even to his ears. He could see why she was angry. He could see why she felt betrayed.

But there was no way he could have told her the real reason she hadn't been let in on his identity: every shred of evidence against the rustlers, every outlaw trail, led straight back to the Lazy S Ranch — and Adam Philips.

Eight

"Did you steal the bull?" Mort asked.

"Yes," Jesse replied.

"Then where is it?" the rustler demanded.

"In a safe place."

"The Boss is waiting for that bull," Mort said. "You were supposed to bring it here." Mort spat chewing tobacco toward the horse trailer he had brought to transport the bull, and which would apparently be leaving empty.

"Plans change," Jesse said.

Mort's eyes narrowed. "What's that supposed to mean?"

Jesse stared right back at the grizzle-faced cowboy. "I've decided to renegotiate the terms of our agreement."

"The Boss ain't gonna like that," Mort warned ominously.

"If he doesn't like it, I can find another buyer for the bull," Jesse said.

"Now hold on a minute," Mort sputtered. "You can't —"

"Tell your boss to be here at midnight tonight," Jesse interrupted. "I'll be waiting with the bull, but I'll only deal with him in person. Tell him the price is double what we agreed on. In cash — small bills."

Mort was clearly alarmed by Jesse's ultimatum. "You're making a big mistake."

"If he wants the bull, he'll come."

It wasn't a subtle method of getting to the top man, Jesse thought, but it inevitably worked. Greed was like that. Of course he would have to watch out for the also inevitable double-cross. There was always the chance that bullets would start flying. He hoped he'd have enough backup to ensure that the guys in the white hats won.

Mort drove away grumbling, and Jesse got into his pickup and headed in the opposite direction from the Flying Diamond. He felt confident that his business for the Rangers would soon be finished. Then he could concentrate on what really mattered — his relationship with Honey. First he had to see Dallas to confirm the details of their plan to capture the brains behind the brawn tonight.

Jesse might have had second thoughts about how soon things were going to be wrapped up if he had known that his visit with Mort Barnes had been observed by another very interested party.

★ ★ ★

Honey was sweeping off the front porch when Adam Philips drove up later that same afternoon. She felt a momentary pang of guilt, but it was quickly followed by relief that she had ended their relationship. Considering they were no longer romantically involved, she couldn't imagine why Adam had come calling.

Honey laid the broom against the wooden wall of the house — noticing that it badly needed another coat of white paint — and stepped over to the porch rail. She held a hand over her brow to keep the sun out of her eyes. "Hello, Adam," she greeted him cautiously. "What brings you out here today?"

It wasn't anything good, Honey surmised after one look at the grim line of Adam's mouth. His features only seemed to get more strained as he left the car and headed up the porch steps toward her.

"Have a seat," Honey said, gesturing toward the wooden swing that hung from the porch rafters. She set a hip on the porch rail, facing the swing.

Adam sat down but abruptly jumped up again and marched over to stand before Honey. "How much do you really know

159

about that man you hired to help around here?"

"Not a lot," Honey admitted with a shrug. "He has a degree in ranch management and —"

"Did it ever occur to you to wonder why a man with a degree in ranch management is content to work as a mere hired hand?" Adam demanded.

Honey stared at him. It hadn't, of course. She hadn't questioned anything about Jesse's story. Which was why his revelation that he was a Texas Ranger had caught her so much off guard. It was clear Adam was still suspicious of Jesse's motives. But there was no reason for him to be. "You don't have to worry about Jesse," she said.

"What makes you so sure?"

"Because he's a Texas Ranger."

"What?" Adam looked stunned.

Honey grinned. "He's working under-cover to catch the rustlers who've been stealing cattle around here. I don't think he'll mind that I told you, but keep it under your hat, okay?"

Adam gave her a sharp look. "Did you know all along that he was a Texas Ranger?"

"I only found out myself this morning," she admitted.

Adam stuck his thumbs into the pockets of his Levi's. He pursed his lips and shook his head ruefully. "Looks like I've been a real fool. I thought that he — Never mind. I'll be going now. I've got some calls to make before dark."

"Adam," Honey called after him.

He stopped and turned back to her. "Yes, Honey?"

"Don't be a stranger."

A pained expression passed fleetingly across his face. He managed a smile and said, "All right. But don't look for me too soon, all right?"

"All right. Goodbye, Adam."

Honey worked alone the rest of the afternoon. She was grateful for Jack's absence because it gave her time to come to terms with Jesse's revelation that he was a Texas Ranger. Equally fortunate, she was spared Jesse's presence as well. He had left earlier to run some errands and hadn't returned.

Maybe it was better that they didn't spend too much time alone. Last night had been a moment out of time, almost too good to be true. It had certainly been too perfect to expect it to last. If only . . .

Honey thought about what she would

have to give up to have Jesse in her life. Having a partner to share the responsibility of the ranch and to be there when she needed him, for one thing. She had sworn when Cale died that she would never marry another man who didn't put her needs, and the needs of the Flying Diamond, at least on an equal footing with his profession.

Although Adam's work as a doctor would have taken him away on occasion, his free time would have been devoted to her. He was wealthy enough to have hired a local man, Chuck Loomis, whose ranch had gone bust, to manage the Lazy S. Honey knew Adam also would have hired the help necessary to take care of the Flying Diamond and preserve it as a heritage for her sons.

Over the past fourteen years, Honey had fought the steady demise of her ranch. But her efforts alone — while Cale had been off fighting badmen — hadn't been enough to make all the repairs needed. The Flying Diamond was a shabby shadow of what it had been in the years when Cale's father had devotedly nurtured it.

She owed it to her sons to marry someone who could help her bring the Flying Diamond back to its former glory.

Jesse could help her make it happen if he devoted himself full-time to running the ranch. But Honey couldn't imagine him being willing to leave the Texas Rangers for any reason, least of all because she asked it of him.

Even if she swallowed her pride and shouldered all the burdens of the Flying Diamond, she would still have to face the constant fear of losing Jesse to an outlaw's bullet. She couldn't bear the constant strain of not knowing whether he would come home to her at the end of the day.

The case Jesse was working on right now was a good example of what she could expect if he didn't quit the Rangers. He had told her the men he was hunting weren't just rustlers, they were murderers. They had killed a rancher in Laredo. If they ever found out a Texas Ranger had insinuated himself in their organization . . . Honey shuddered at the thought of what would happen to Jesse.

She hadn't forgotten what it felt like when she'd heard that Cale had been killed in the line of duty. She didn't ever want to suffer through that kind of anguish again. In the few weeks he had been around, Jesse had made a place for himself in her life and in her heart. She didn't want to contemplate how she would suffer if something went wrong and he was killed.

"Penny for your thoughts?"

Honey nearly fell backward over the porch rail. Jesse reached out and caught her, pulling her into his embrace. Honey's arms circled his broad shoulders and she looked into his amused face.

"Nearly lost you," he said. "What were you daydreaming about?"

She wasn't about to admit she had been worrying about him. "I was just thinking what good weather Jack has for tubing on the river."

"You mean he's not home yet?"

"No," she said, embarrassed by how breathless her voice sounded. Honey flushed at the intent look on Jesse's face as it suddenly dawned on him that they had the place to themselves. She swallowed hard and said, "Where have you been all day?"

"Doing business for the Texas Rangers," he admitted. "But I'm all yours now."

The leer on his face made it plain what he hoped she would do with him.

Honey was tempted to start a fight, or do whatever else was necessary to make Jesse angry enough to leave her alone. On the other hand, she was also very much

164

aware of the sensual lure he had thrown out to her. Their time together was coming to a close. It was hard to say no when he was here, wanting her, desiring her, with his eyes and his voice and his body.

He reached out and tugged on the waist-band of her jeans. The top button popped free.

"Don't even think it," she warned.

"You can read my mind?"

"Enough to know you're crazy."

"Probably certifiable," he admitted. "But if you don't tell, I won't."

He made growling sounds and bit her neck, sending a frisson of fire through her veins.

She grabbed Jesse's face to try to make him stop whatever tantalizing thing he was doing to her throat with his tongue, but he caught her hands and forced them behind her. Twining their fingers together, he used them to pull her between his widespread legs where his arousal was evident.

"Jesse," she protested with a breathless laugh. "We can't. It's broad daylight."

"There's no one to see," he said, thrusting against her and causing her to groan as her body responded to the ur-gency of his.

She was running out of excuses for him

not to do what she so desperately wanted him to do. "Jack might come home."

"Then we'll just have to go where he won't find us," Jesse murmured conspiratorially.

Honey thought he meant her bedroom, but he obviously had other ideas. She gasped when he threw her over his shoulder and headed for the barn.

"Not the barn!" she hooted.

"Why not the barn?" he said with a grin.

"Hay itches."

He stopped and rearranged her in his arms so he could see her face. "Sounds like you speak from experience."

The color rose on Honey's cheeks. When Jesse laughed she hid her face against his throat.

He murmured in her ear, "If you feel any itches anywhere I'll be glad to scratch them."

Honey giggled like a schoolgirl. She felt so carefree! If only it could always be like this, laughter and loving, with no thought of the future to spoil it. Honey nibbled on Jesse's ear and heard him hiss in a breath of air.

"Keep that up, woman, and we won't make it to the barn," he warned.

Honey was feeling in a dangerous mood.

She teased his ear with her tongue, tracing the shell-like shape of it. She shrieked when Jesse teasingly threatened to drop her.

At the barn door he stopped and stood her before him so he could look at her.

When Honey caught sight of his face she knew she was playing with fire. His dark eyes were heavy-lidded, his features taut with desire. His nostrils flared and his hands tightened on her flesh. Her whole body tensed in response to his obvious sexual hunger.

Her fingertips caressed his cheekbones and slid up from his temple into the thick black hair at his nape. "I want you, Jesse."

Her words were like a match on tinder. Jesse's mouth came down on hers, his tongue thrusting in a mirror image of that age-old dance between men and women. Her fingers clutched at his hair, forcing his hat off his head. She grabbed hold of him as though to keep from flying off into the unknown. For nothing Jesse did to her from then on was like anything that had ever happened to her before.

His mouth found her nipple through her thin cotton shirt, rousing her to passion. His hand slid down the front of her jeans and cupped the heat and heart of her. He urged her hand down to the hard bulge that threatened the seams of his Levi's. He thrust against her, his desire a stronger aphrodisiac than any shaman's love potion.

They stood just inside the barn door, and Jesse molded them together belly to belly as he backed her out of the sunlight and into the shadows. "It's time you and I had a talk about what happens when you tease a man," Jesse rasped, pressing her up against the barn wall with his body.

He insinuated his thigh between her legs and lifted her so she could feel the heat and pressure of his flesh against that most sensitive of feminine places. Meanwhile he cupped a breast in one hand while the other captured her nape to hold her still for the onslaught of his mouth and the invasion of his tongue.

"Honey," he rasped. "I can't get enough of you, the feel of you, the taste of you."

Honey was overwhelmed. She couldn't breathe. She couldn't move. She could only respond to the sensations that assaulted her. Her knees collapsed and Jesse had to hold her upright.

Abruptly he left her and she leaned against the rough wooden walls, legs outstretched, while he grabbed a clean saddle blanket and spread it hurriedly over the fresh, crackling straw in an empty stall at the back of the barn.

She felt his urgency as he returned to lift her into his arms and carry her to the blanket, laying her down carefully before mantling her with his body.

Honey looked up into eyes that were narrowed in concentration on her, fierce, dark eyes that should have frightened her but only made her wild with anticipation.

Slowly, slowly, Jesse began unbuttoning her shirt. His mouth caressed her flesh as he exposed it, until he reached the button on her Levi's. The button hardly made a sound as it fell free, but her zipper grated noisily as he slid it down. His mouth followed where his hands had led and soon he was nuzzling at the very apex of her thighs.

Honey reached for whatever part of him she could grasp, but when he nipped her through her silken panties her nails curved into the muscles of his back.

"Jesse!"

He sat up to pull off her boots and then his own. She yanked off her socks and then his, grinning at the sight of his long naked feet. He started to unsnap his shirt, but she stopped him.

"Let me."

She offered him the same enjoyment he had given her, exposing his bronze skin one snap at a time and caressing it with her lips and tongue. Intrigued by his distended nipples she forayed across his chest to nibble gently on one.

His whole body tensed, and he held himself motionless while she tested his control. He didn't last long. A moment later she found herself flat on her back, Jesse astride her.

"Play with fire and you can get burned, woman."

He unsnapped the front clasp of her bra and brushed it aside as he took one of her nipples in his mouth to tease it with his tongue. Honey arched upward with her hips and encountered the hardness of his arousal.

She grasped his buttocks to pull him close and spread her legs to accommodate him more fully. Jesse returned the pressure as she gently rubbed herself against him.

Abruptly Jesse freed himself from her grasp and began stripping her. She was equally urgent in her efforts to undress him until moments later they stared at each other in the filtered sunlight.

"God, you're beautiful," he said reverently.

Honey felt herself flushing with pleasure at the compliment. She knew he wasn't merely mouthing the words. His delight was mirrored in his eyes.

"I'm glad I please you."

The gentle touch of his mouth on hers was like a paean to a goddess. He honored her. He revered her. He desired her. His lips and mouth and tongue adored her. The kisses that began at her mouth continued downward to her throat, found their way to her breasts, then to her belly and beyond.

Honey stiffened and reached out a hand to grip his shoulder. She hadn't expected this. She wasn't sure whether she wanted it.

Jesse raised his eyes to hers. "I want to taste all of you," he said.

In all the years they had been married, Cale had never loved her this way. It was the most intimate of kisses. And it required complete trust. Jesse was aware of that, and he awaited her consent. Honey was wired as tight as a bowstring, anxious to please him, afraid she wouldn't, afraid of the unknown. Of that forbidden pleasure.

She had always wondered what it would feel like, always wondered whether it truly brought the immeasurable ecstasy that made it something to be whispered about. All she had to do was trust Jesse enough to allow him to love her as he so clearly wanted to do.

She opened her mouth to agree, but no sound came out. She swallowed hard and slowly nodded her head.

Jesse's quick grin surprised her. "You won't be sorry," he said. Just as quickly the grin disappeared. "You only have to say the word and I'll stop. This is supposed to please us both. All right?"

Honey nodded again.

She was surprised when he rose and kissed her on the mouth again. He took his time kissing his way back down her body, but she knew where he was heading. By the time he got there she was more aroused than she could ever remember being.

For Jesse had not relied on his mouth alone to make that journey. His callused hands had smoothed across her flesh, finding her breasts and teasing them, taunting her by rolling her nipples between fingers and thumb. He had caressed ribs and hipbones and the length of her back from her nape to the dimples at the curve of her spine. She was sure she would find impressions of his fingers on her buttocks where he had lazily learned the shape of them.

Finally he lifted her in his hands while his tongue teased her. She gasped as her body tautened. She grabbed handfuls of the wool blanket to keep from touching him, lest he think she wanted him to stop. For she didn't. Oh, no, she did not!

Honey felt the ripples building, felt her inner flesh clenching, felt the muscles in her thighs tighten until she could not move. And still he kissed her. Loved her. Teased her with his mouth and tongue.

She moaned and writhed in pleasure. Her body arched toward him and at last her hands reached for him, clutching at his shoulders as though he could save her from the cataclysmic — wondrous, astounding, remarkable — things her body threatened to do.

Honey did not want to let go of what little control she had left. There was no hiding the strong muscular contractions as she began climaxing beneath him. Excited, animal sounds came from her throat as she convulsed with pleasure.

Jesse met her eyes and watched the agony of ecstasy that she could not hide from him.

When it was over, she turned her face

away from him. Her throat was swollen with emotion and tears stung her eyes.

"Honey?"

She heard the anxiety in his voice and tried to reassure him. But no sound would pass over the lump in her throat. She reached out and grasped his hand.

He lay down beside her and brushed a sweat-dampened lock of hair from her brow. "Are you all right?"

She nodded jerkily.

"You're not acting all right," he said.

She hid her face in his throat and clutched him around the waist.

He continued smoothing her hair and rubbing her back gently. She couldn't see his face, but she could feel from the tension in his body that he was troubled. She wanted to reassure him that she was all right, but she was simply so *overwhelmed* by what had happened that words did not seem sufficient to explain how she felt.

Eventually her breathing calmed and her throat relaxed. "It was so . . ."

Jesse put a finger under her chin and forced her eyes up to meet his. "So what?"

"Beautiful," she whispered.

He hugged her hard then and rocked her back and forth. "I'm glad," he said. "I'm so glad. I was afraid —"

"It was wonderful," she said. Then, shyly, "I only hope you're going to give me the pleasure of returning the favor."

He grinned. "Someday soon," he promised. "Right now, there's something more I want from you."

"What's that?"

"This."

He nudged her knees apart and sheathed himself easily in her still half-aroused body.

When he kissed her again, Honey found the taste of herself still on his lips. She gave back to him that which he had given her. She was far beyond rational thought by that time, only wanting to join herself with him in any way she could.

Honey touched Jesse's body everywhere she could reach as he sought to bring her to a second pinnacle of pleasure. She wasn't really conscious of how she caressed him, but moved her hands in response to the way he arched his sinewy body beneath her, the way he moved toward her touch or away from it. By sheer luck she found a spot — the crease where belly met thigh — that made him shudder with pleasure.

Jesse did not allow her time to tarry. He lifted her legs up over his thighs and took them both on a journey of delight. After she had fallen off the world yet again, he poured his seed into her, his head arched back in ecstasy, every muscle taut with unspeakable pleasure.

Afterward, they both slept. It was nearly dark by the time Honey wakened. Jesse's head rested on his hand and he was staring down at her as though memorizing her features.

"It's late," she said.

"We'd better get dressed," he agreed.

Neither of them moved.

"After tonight, I'll be finished with my work here," Jesse said at last.

Honey closed her eyes to hide the myriad emotions vying for dominance. "When will you be leaving?"

"Honey, I . . ."

She opened her eyes. "I'll miss you," she admitted. She reached up to touch his mouth with a fingertip. Was she responsible for the sensuous look of his swollen lower lip?

He took her hand in his and kissed each finger. "I love you, Honey. Will you marry me?"

Honey was so shocked her mouth fell open.

He nudged at her chin with a bent finger. "Catch a lot of flies that way," he teased in a husky voice.

But Honey saw how his hand trembled when he took it away. It was clear that despite his levity he cared a great deal about how she answered. She was so tempted to say yes! But it wasn't fair to marry Jesse without expressing the reservations she harbored.

"Are you willing to quit the Rangers?" she asked.

"Are you making that a condition of your acceptance?" he answered in a sharp voice.

Honey took a deep breath and said, "Yes, I think I am."

He was on his feet an instant later, pulling on his pants. "That's totally unreasonable, Honey, and you know it!" he ranted.

She was suddenly embarrassed to be naked when he was dressed. She grabbed at her shirt and stuck her arms into the sleeves. Honey searched for her panties and found them across the stall. She turned her back on Jesse to step into them and was conscious of the silence as she did. Over her shoulder she discovered him ogling her bottom.

She yanked her panties on and dragged her jeans over her legs. "I don't see what's so unreasonable about wanting a husband who'll be around to help run this ranch!"

"I'd be around!" he insisted.

"In between assignments," she retorted. "You forget, I've already been married to one Texas Ranger. You're as bad as Cale."

"Don't tar me with the same brush."

"How are you different?" she demanded. "You can't deny you take the same foolish, dangerous chances with your life that he did. And look what happened to him! I couldn't bear it if —"

Honey cut herself off and went searching for her socks.

Jesse grabbed her by the arms and forced her to face him. "I know you love me," he began.

"That isn't the point," Honey interrupted.

"Then you do love me?"

He stood there waiting for an answer. Honey grimaced and admitted, "I love you but —"

Jesse cut her off with a hard kiss. "Then all the rest is small stuff. We can work it out."

"You're not listening to me," Honey said, her voice rising as she felt control of the situation slipping away. "I won't marry you, Jesse. Not unless you're willing to give up the Rangers."

His mouth thinned in anger. "You're asking the impossible."

"Why is it impossible? There are other challenges in life besides hunting down outlaws."

"Like what?"

"Like raising kids. Like making a success of this ramshackle ranch. Like growing a garden. Like spending the afternoon making sweet, sweet love to your wife."

He captured her in his arms and nuzzled her throat. "The last part of that certainly sounds promising."

Honey remained stiff in his embrace, fighting the tears that threatened. *"Listen to me,"* she pleaded. "I'm fighting for our life together."

His head jerked up and he glared down at her. "So am I," he insisted. "You're asking me to give up what I *am*."

Honey shook her head sadly. "No, Jesse. It's just a job. You can quit."

"And if I won't?"

She pushed at his shoulders, forcing him to release her. "Then I guess this is goodbye."

His lips flattened. "You don't mean that."

Her chin lifted and her shoulders

squared. "Goodbye, Jesse."

She turned and marched barefoot from the barn, leaving Jesse to stare at her stiff back.

"Damned fool woman," he muttered. "Can't expect me to give up everything for her. She's crazy if she thinks I will. No woman is worth that kind of sacrifice."

It was a sober and contemplative man who left the barn. The best thing to do was put the situation with Honey out of his mind and concentrate on his rendezvous with the rustlers. It wouldn't do to let himself get distracted. Honey was right about one thing. A Texas Ranger led a dangerous life. He had to pay attention to what he was doing tonight or he might end up getting himself killed. He snorted in disgust. He would hate like hell to prove Honey right about the dangers of his job.

Nine

Because of all she had been through with Jesse, Honey hadn't given Jack a thought for the past twenty-four hours. In fact, she had spent most of that time in a euphoric haze. Memories of Jesse's lovemaking had preoccupied her in the morning, and their interlude in the barn, his proposal and their subsequent quarrel had kept her agitated until well after dark. It wasn't until nearly nine o'clock Saturday evening that she realized how late Jack was in returning home and began making inquiries.

Honey was aghast when she discovered Jack had not spent the night with a friend — or even made plans to do so. He hadn't gone tubing on the Frio, either! Jack had never lied to her before. She couldn't imagine where he could have gone last night, unless . . .

The worst conclusion to be drawn from the facts came first: *Jack had run away from home.* Honey suddenly remembered how hard Jack had hugged her last night before he left the house, how intently he had looked into her eyes. She hadn't paid much attention to the hug except to be pleased by it because Jack so seldom indulged in such sentimentality these days. Now his hug took on ominous significance. *Jack had been saying goodbye!*

Honey's heart began thudding heavily. Her palms tingled. She felt light-headed. Her knees went weak and she had to sit down before she fell down.

Things had been rough for the past year since Cale's death, but surely not bad enough for her son to want to escape the situation. Jesse's appearance had injected a note of tension in the household, but Jack seemed to have made his peace with Jesse the day they worked together on the corral.

But maybe Jack had only been pretending things were all right. Maybe he had resented the hired hand much more than he had let on. Maybe having his mother courted by two men at the same time was more strain than he could handle. But he didn't have to run away!

To Honey's chagrin, the first person she thought of to help her hunt for Jack was Jesse Whitelaw. But shortly after their argument in the barn, Jesse had gotten into his pickup and driven away. Honey didn't know where. And she didn't care.

Honey snickered in disgust. Who was

she trying to kid? She cared. She already missed Jesse and he hadn't even left the Flying Diamond. At least, she didn't think he was gone for good. His things were still in the small room off the kitchen. She knew because she had checked.

Honey shuddered to think that the man she loved had been in any way responsible for her son running away from home. What an awful mess her life had become!

Well, she would just have to straighten it out. Jack had to learn he couldn't run from his problems, that he had to confront them head-on and resolve them. And Jesse, well, he could stand to learn a lesson or two about not running from problems himself. She was just the woman to instruct them both!

Deciding she could use reinforcements, Honey picked up the phone and called Dallas Masterson. Angel answered.

"Is Dallas there?" Honey asked.

"I'm afraid he's gone for the evening. Some Ranger business," Angel said.

Honey had completely forgotten about General and the trap Jesse was supposedly laying for the rustlers. Was that where he was tonight? Was his life in danger even now?

"Honey, are you okay?" Angel asked,

concerned by the long silence.

Honey sank back into a kitchen chair. "I don't think so."

"What's wrong? Can I help?"

"Jack's missing," Honey said. "And I don't have the first clue where to look for him."

"I'll be right over," Angel said.

"What about the baby?"

"I'll bring him. He'll be fine riding in the car while we look for Jack. Don't go anywhere till I get there. I won't be long."

"I'll use the time to call some more of Jack's friends. Maybe they'll have some idea where he is," Honey said.

Angel was as good as her word, and a short while later she drove into the yard. Honey came running out and jumped into the passenger's side of the car.

"Do you have any suggestions where we can start looking?" Angel asked.

"No," Honey said. She bit down on her lower lip to still its tremor. "We might as well start on the Flying Diamond. Maybe he —" Honey stopped herself from saying *had an accident;* it was a possibility she didn't want to consider. It was almost better believing he had run away.

They searched the Flying Diamond in vain. Jack was nowhere to be found. Honey was getting frantic. It was nearly midnight. *Where was her son?*

"I don't know where to look from here, except to check whether he might have gone to see Adam at the Lazy S," Honey said at last.

"Dallas told me to stay away from the Lazy S tonight. There's something going on at that corral where your boys practiced roping earlier this spring."

"As I recall, there's a pen for livestock," Honey said, thinking aloud. "So that's where Jesse hid General!"

"What are you talking about?" Angel asked.

"Last night Jesse stole General."

"What!"

"It's a long story. Anyway, he said he'd put him somewhere safe. I'm betting he meant the pen at that roundup corral on the southern border of the Lazy S. If Dallas told you to stay away from there tonight —"

"— because of Ranger business —"

"— then chances are that's where they both are right now." Honey hissed in a breath of air. "Jack couldn't have suspected . . . he wouldn't have gone . . . Jack just couldn't . . ."

"Jack couldn't what?" Angel asked.

Honey had a terrible feeling of foreboding. "We have to get to that corral," she said. "Hurry!"

"Dallas specifically said to stay away from there," Angel protested.

"Jack's there!" Honey said.

"How do you know?"

"Call it a mother's instinct if you like, but he's there, all right, and he's in trouble! Let's go!"

Jack hadn't liked lying to his mother, but sometimes there were things a man had to do. Protecting his mother was one of those things. So he had told her he was spending the night with a friend and asked if it was all right to spend the following day tubing on the Frio River. In reality, he planned to spend the entire time spying on Jesse Whitelaw.

Jack had grudgingly given Jesse the benefit of the doubt after their talk in the barn. By the end of a day spent working with the hired hand, he had felt a secret admiration for the cowboy. Then he had overheard Jesse on the phone after dinner, making plans to rent a stock trailer.

At first Jack supposed his mother had sold some cattle. When Jesse mentioned something about "restraints for the bull,"

186

Jack got suspicious. There was only one bull on the Flying Diamond, and General wasn't for sale. Jack felt sick.

He had secretly been dreaming about what it would be like if Jesse Whitelaw became his stepfather. He had imagined lots of days like the one they had spent together working to repair the corral. Jesse had treated him as an equal. He had respected him as a person. Working with Jesse hadn't been a chore, it had been fun.

Now Jack saw Jesse's behavior as a phony act to lull him and his mother into complacency, so they wouldn't interfere when Jesse stole the one thing of true value left on the Flying Diamond. Jack felt like a fool. The more he thought about it, the angrier he got, until there seemed only one course of action open to him. He would catch Jesse Whitelaw red-handed. He would put the deceitful drifter in jail where he would have plenty of time to regret having underestimated a gullible, trusting, thirteen-year-old boy.

Jack had packed an overnight bag and hugged his mom goodbye as though he were spending the night with friends. Instead, he had hidden himself where he could stand guard on the barn. Sure enough, about an hour after his mother left the house with Adam Philips, Jesse Whitelaw had backed a stock trailer up to the barn and let down the ramp.

At first Jack had been tempted to confront the drifter. But even at his age he knew discretion was the better part of valor. He thought about running to the house to call the police, but figured Jesse would be long gone before anyone could block the roads leading from the Flying Diamond.

So while Jesse was in the barn with the bull, Jack had snuck under a tarp lying in the back of the pickup truck pulling the stock trailer. It was all very easy, and Jack was pleased with how clever he had been. Surprisingly, Jesse had taken the bull to the roundup corral on the southern edge of the Lazy S.

Jack knew he ought to go right to his mother with what information he had, but he was afraid she would let Jesse go because of her soppy feelings for the drifter. So while Jesse was unloading the bull into one of the stock pens, Jack left the truck and hid inside a nearby tin-roofed shed, figuring he couldn't go wrong staying with General. Besides, if he left, the bull might be gone by the time he got back with the authorities.

Jack was nearly discovered when Jesse came inside the shed to get hay for the bull. Apparently the theft had been more well thought out than Jack had realized. To Jack's dismay, when Jesse left the shed he dropped a wooden bar across the door. *Jack was trapped!*

His first instinct was to call out. Fear kept him silent. There was no telling what the drifter would do if he knew he had been found out. Jack remained quiet as the truck drove away. Surely Jesse would return soon. All Jack had to do was wait and be sure he got out of the shed undetected when it was opened again.

Jack had spent a long, uncomfortable night on a pile of prickly hay. He had finally fallen asleep in the wee hours of the morning and only wakened when the sun was high in the sky. He was relieved to see through a knothole in the wooden-sided shed that General was still in the stock pen, but he was also confused. Surely someone should have come to collect the bull by now.

All day long, Jack waited expectantly for Jesse to return. It was late afternoon by the time he realized the exchange would likely be made after dark. He was hot and hungry and thirsty and dearly regretted not having called the police when he had first had an inkling of what Jesse intended.

Jack wondered whether his mother had checked up on him and uncovered his lies. He consoled himself with the thought that she wouldn't really start to worry until after dark. Only the sun had fallen hours ago. Where was she? Why hadn't anybody come looking for him? Where was Jesse? *Where was everybody?*

Jesse hunkered down in the ravine where Dallas was hidden so he wouldn't be spotted talking to the other Ranger. "Is everything set?" he asked.

"The local police have the entire area covered like a glove," Dallas reassured him.

"I just hope Adam steps into the trap," Jesse said.

Dallas shook his head. "He isn't going to be the one who shows up here tonight. You'll see. I'd stake my life on it."

Jesse arched a disbelieving brow. "You're still sticking by the man, even with all the evidence we have leading to the Lazy S? With all we've discovered about how his ranch has floundered lately? With everything we know about how bad Adam Philips's finances have gotten over the past year?"

Dallas nodded. "I know Adam. He just can't be involved in something like this. There's got to be another explanation."

"For your sake, I hope you're right," Jesse said. But he wouldn't mind if Adam Philips ended up being a villain in Honey's eyes. Maybe then she would start to see Jesse in a more positive light.

That woman was the most stubborn, bullheaded, downright maddening creature Jesse had ever known. How he had fallen so deeply in love with her was a mystery to him, but the fact was, he had. Now the fool woman was refusing to marry him unless he left the Rangers. Damn her willful hide!

He couldn't possibly give up an honor he had striven so hard to achieve. Why, the Rangers were an elite group of men. Independent. Fearless. Ruthless when necessary. He was proud to be part of such an historic organization. It was unfair of Honey to ask him to make such a sacrifice.

Yet he could see her side of the issue. Over the weeks he had worked on the Flying Diamond, he had gotten a glimmer of how little time Cale Farrell had devoted to the place. It wasn't just the roof that needed repair, or a few rotten corral posts that had to be replaced. The whole ranch showed signs of serious neglect.

It was apparent that because of Cale's commitment to the Rangers, the brunt of the ranch work must have fallen on Honey's shoulders. Not that they weren't lovely shoulders, but they weren't strong enough to support the entire weight of an outfit the size of the Flying Diamond.

Jesse had seen dozens of opportunities where better management — and plain hard work — would have improved the yield of the ranch. The Flying Diamond had land that could be put to use growing feed. Expanded, Honey's vegetable garden could easily provide for the needs of the ranch. And it wouldn't be a bad idea to invest in some mohair goats. The money from the mohair harvest could be applied to supporting the cattle end of the ranch.

If he stayed on as a Ranger, Jesse wouldn't have much time to invest in the ranch. He could expect to be called away on assignments often. Honey would be left to take care of things. As she must have been left for most of her married life, Jesse suddenly realized.

He had never heard Honey complain once about the burden she had carried all these years. And he was only thinking in terms of the ranch. Honey had probably borne most of the responsibility as a parent as well. She had done a good job. Jack and Jonathan were fine boys that any man would be proud to call sons.

Jesse felt a tightness in his chest when he remembered the look he and Jack had shared at the end of the day they had spent working together. Jesse had never known a stronger feeling of satisfaction. He had truly felt close to the boy. It was hard to imagine walking away from Jack and Jonathan. It was impossible to imagine walking away from Honey.

All his life Jesse had somehow managed to have his cake and eat it, too. Honey was asking him to make a choice. He just didn't know what it was going to be.

Jesse saw the truck lights in the distance and checked the revolver he had stuck in the back of his jeans. It wasn't particularly easy to get to, but then, he was hoping the show of force by the police would reduce the chance of gunplay. He stood by the corral waiting as the tractor-trailer truck pulled up. The engine remained running. It was Mort Barnes who stepped into the glare of the truck headlights.

Jesse stiffened. He saw his efforts to finally uncover the man in charge going up in smoke. "Where's your boss?" he demanded.

Mort grinned, though it looked more like a sneer. "I'm the boss."

"I don't believe you," Jesse said flatly.

Mort revealed the automatic weapon in his hand and said, "I'll take that bull."

Jesse didn't hesitate. He threw himself out of the light at the same instant Mort fired. Instead of running for cover, Jesse leapt toward the rustler. Blinded by the headlights, Mort didn't see Jesse until he had been knocked down and his gun kicked out of his hand, disappearing somewhere in the underbrush.

Moments later, Jesse straddled Mort on the ground, with a viselike grip on the rustler's throat and his gun aimed at the rustler's head. "I told you I'm only going to deal with your boss."

"Why you —" Mort rasped.

"You can release Mort," a voice said from the shadows on the other side of the truck, "and drop the gun. I'm here."

Jesse didn't recognize the man who stepped into view, his automatic weapon aimed at the center of Jesse's back. But it wasn't Adam Philips. Jesse dropped his gun. Then he released Mort and stood to face the newest threat. "Are you the boss of this outfit?"

"I am," the man said. "I can't say it's a

pleasure to meet you, Mr. Whitelaw. Actually, you've thrown a bit of a cork-screw into my plans. If you'll just step over to that shed, we can finish our business."

"You brought the money?" Jesse asked.

"Oh, no. All deals are off. I'm simply offering you a chance to get out of this alive. Are you going to walk over there peacefully, or not? I've already killed once. I assure you I won't hesitate to do so again."

Jesse was pretty sure the Boss intended to kill him anyway, but he was counting on Dallas to make sure he got out of this alive. Meanwhile, he had best keep his wits about him. He took his time sliding away the board that held the shed door closed, giving Dallas plenty of time to get everybody into position. Once Jesse was inside the shed and, he hoped, before the Boss man shot him, Dallas would move and it would all be over.

The instant Jesse released the door, a blur of movement shot past him. The escaping body was caught by Mort. Jesse's blood froze when he saw the gangly teenager the rustler was wrestling into submission.

"What the hell are you doing here?" Jesse rasped.

"Waiting for you!" Jack retorted. "You

won't get away with this, you know. I'll tell them everything. They'll catch you, and you'll go to jail forever."

"Dammit, Jack, I —"

"Hey!" Jack was eyeing the man holding the gun on Jesse. "I know you! You're the foreman of the Lazy S. What're you doing here, Mr. Loomis?"

"Dammit, Jack," Jesse muttered. Now the fat was in the fire.

"You got any more surprises hidden around here?" Loomis asked Jesse.

"Look, the kid being here is as much a surprise to me as it is to you," Jesse said.

Jesse closely watched the man Jack had identified as Mr. Loomis and saw his mouth tighten, his eyes narrow. By identifying the Boss and making threats of going to the law, Jack had signed his own death warrant. Jesse forced himself not to glance out into the darkness. Adam's foreman was suspicious enough already. Dallas would realize that the boy's presence complicated things and make new plans accordingly.

"Both of you get into the shed," Loomis said, gesturing with the gun.

Jack spied the gun for the first time, and his eyes slid to Jesse's, wide with fright.

"It's all right," Jesse said in a voice intended to calm the youth. "They're just going to lock us up in the shed."

Jesse's last doubts that Loomis intended killing them both ended when Mort chuckled maliciously and said, "Yeah, you two just mosey on inside."

Jack struggled against Mort's hold, and the outlaw slapped him hard. "Quit your bellyachin' and get movin'."

Jesse had decided to use the distraction Jack was creating to make a lunge for Loomis's gun, when a pair of headlights appeared on the horizon.

"I knew it was a trap!" the outlaw snarled. Loomis swung the gun around to aim it at Jack and fired just as Jesse grabbed at his hand, pulling it down.

Jesse grunted as the bullet plowed into his thigh, but he never let go of his hold on Loomis's wrist. He swung a fist at the foreman's face and heard a satisfying crunch as it connected with the man's hooked nose. Loomis managed to fire once more before Jesse wrenched the gun away, but the bullet drove harmlessly into the ground.

Moments later, the area was swarming with local police and Texas Rangers. It soon became apparent to Jack from the way Dallas Masterson greeted Jesse, that the drifter wasn't going to be arrested by

197

the Texas Rangers *because he was one!*

"What idiot turned on those head-lights?" Jesse demanded. "Damned near got us killed!"

Jesse's head jerked up when he heard the sound of a woman's voice beyond the arc of light provided by the semi's headlights. "Who's that?"

Dallas grinned. "The idiot who turned on the headlights."

Jesse only had a second to brace himself before Honey threw herself into his arms. Her eyes were white around the rims with fright. Her whole body was shaking.

"I saw what happened. You saved Jack's life! I heard shots. Are you hurt?" She pushed herself away to look at him and saw the dark shine of blood on his leg. "My God! You've been shot!" She turned to the crowd of men scattered over the area and shouted, "Where's a doctor? Why haven't you taken this man to the hospital?"

Jesse pulled her back into his arms. "It's all right, Honey. It's just a little flesh wound. I'll be fine."

Jack stepped into the light and stood nearby, afraid to approach his mother and the drifter . . . who wasn't really a drifter after all.

Honey saw her son and reached out to

pull him close. "Are you all right? You're not hurt?"

"I'm fine," Jack mumbled, feeling lower than a worm for having caused so much trouble.

"You're damned lucky not to be dead!" Jesse said.

Jack glared at Jesse. "If you'd just told me the truth in the first place, none of this would have happened. I spent a whole day in that stupid shed for nothing!" He turned to his mother and said, "I'm hungry. Is there anything at home to eat?"

Honey gaped at Jack and then laughed. If her son had started thinking about his stomach, he was going to be just fine.

Dallas had left briefly and now joined them again. "I've got a car to take you to the hospital, Jesse."

"I'll see you at home, Honey," Jesse said.

Now that she knew Jesse was all right, Honey forced herself to step away from him. If anything, this episode only proved what she had known all along. She didn't want to be married to a Texas Ranger. "I'll let you in to get your things," she said. "But I expect you to find somewhere else to spend what's left of the night."

Jesse didn't argue, just limped away toward the car Dallas had waiting.

But Jack wasn't about to let the subject alone. "He saved my life, Mom."

"I suppose he did."

"You can't just throw him out of the house like that."

"I can and I will."

"If you want my opinion, I think you're making a mistake," Jack said.

"I didn't ask for your opinion," Honey said. "Besides, you've got a lot to answer for yourself, young man."

Jack grimaced. "I can explain everything."

"This I've got to hear."

Angel interrupted to say, "I can give you both a ride home now."

"Let's go," Honey said. She put her arm around Jack and dared him to try to slip out from under it. "It's been a hectic night. Let's go home and get some sleep."

"But I'm hungry!" Jack protested.

"All right. First you eat. Then it's bed for both of us."

But hours later — just before dawn — when Jesse Whitelaw returned, Honey was sitting in the kitchen, coffee cup in hand, waiting for him.

Ten

Honey didn't move when the kitchen door opened, just waited for Jesse to come to her. Her eyes drifted closed when his hands clasped her shoulders. She exhaled with a soughing sigh. He didn't give her a chance to object, just hauled her out of the chair, turned her into his arms and held her tight.

Honey's arms slipped around his waist and clutched his shirt. Her nose slipped into the hollow at his throat and she inhaled the sweaty man-scent that was his and his alone. She wanted to remember it when he was gone. And she *was* going to send him away.

"We have to talk," Jesse whispered in her ear.

Honey gripped him tighter, knowing she had to let him go. "I think I've said everything I have to say."

"I haven't." His lips twisted wryly. "I think this is where I'm supposed to sweep you into my arms and carry you off to the bedroom," he said. "But I don't think my leg could stand the strain."

Honey realized all at once how heavily

he was leaning on her. "Come sit down," she said, urging him toward a kitchen chair.

"Let's find something a little more comfortable," he said. "Getting up and down is a pain. I'd like to find someplace I can stay awhile."

She slipped an arm around his waist to support him while he put an arm across her shoulders. Slowly they made their way to the living room, where he levered himself onto the brass-studded leather couch. He winced as she helped him lift both legs and stretch out full-length.

She knelt beside him on the polished hardwood floor.

Jesse took one of her hands in both of his and brought it to his lips. He kissed each fingertip and then the palm of her hand. He laid her hand against his cheek, bristly now with a day's growth of beard, and turned to gaze into her eyes.

"Let me stay here tonight," he said.

"Jesse, I don't think —"

"We have to talk, Honey, but I can barely keep my eyes open."

"You can't stay here," she said. If he did, she would be tempted to let him stay another night, and another. Before she knew it, he would be a permanent fixture. "You have to leave," she insisted.

He smiled wearily. "Sorry. I'm afraid that's out of the question. Can't seem to get a muscle to move anywhere." His eyes drifted closed. "I have some things to say . . ."

He was asleep.

Honey stared at the beloved face before her and felt her heart wrench in her breast. How could she let him stay? How could she make him go?

She sighed and rose to find a blanket. After all, it was only one night. She would be able to argue with him better once she had gotten some sleep herself.

The homemade quilt barely reached from one end to the other of the tall Ranger. Jesse's face was gentle in repose. There was no hint of the fierceness in battle she had seen, no hint of the savage passion she had experienced. He was only a man. There must be another — not a Ranger — who would suit her as well.

She leaned down slowly, carefully, and touched her lips to his. A goodbye kiss. She walked dry-eyed up the stairs to her bedroom. It looked so empty. It felt so forlorn. She lay down on the bed and stared at the canopy overhead. It was a long time before she finally found respite in sleep.

The sun woke Honey the next morning. It was brighter than bright, a golden Texas morning. Honey stretched and groaned at how stiff she felt. Then she froze. Where was Jesse now?

Was he still downstairs sleeping? Had he packed and left? Was he dressed and waiting to confront her?

Honey scrambled off the bed and ran across the hall to the bathroom. She took one look at herself and groaned. Her face looked as if she'd slept in it. She started the water running in the tub as hot as she could get it and stripped off her clothes. There was barely an inch of liquid in the claw-footed tub by the time she stepped into it. She sank down, hissing as the water scalded her, then grabbed a cloth and began soaping herself clean.

It never occurred to her to lock the bathroom door. No one ever bothered her when she was in the bathroom. Her eyes widened in surprise when the door opened and Jesse sauntered in. He was shirtless, wearing a pair of jeans that threatened to fall off, revealing his navel and the beginning of his hipbones.

She held the washcloth in front of her, which didn't do much good, not to mention how silly it looked. "What are you

204

doing in here?" she demanded indignantly.

"I thought I'd shave," Jesse said. "We might as well get used to having to share the bathroom in the morning." He turned and grinned. "That is, unless I can talk you into adding a second bathroom. One with a *shower?*"

"What's going on, Jesse?"

He soaped up his shaving brush and began applying the resulting foam to his beard. "I'm shaving," he answered. "Looks like you're taking a bath." He grinned.

Honey tried ignoring him. She turned her back on him and continued washing herself. She was feeling both angry and confused. *He has no right to be doing this! Why doesn't he just go?* If Jesse had changed his mind about leaving the Rangers he would have told her so last night. This was just another ploy to get his own way. She wasn't going to let him get away with it.

Honey covered herself with the washcloth as best she could while she reached for a towel. Just as she caught it with her fingertips, Jesse slipped it off the rack and settled it around his neck.

"I need that towel," she said through gritted teeth.

"I'll be done with it in a minute," he

said. "I need to wipe off the excess shaving cream."

Honey was tempted to stand up and stroll past him naked, but she didn't have the nerve. What if Jack was out there? *Jack!*

"Where's Jack?" she asked.

"Sent him out to round up those steers we vaccinated and move them to another pasture."

"And he went?"

"Don't look so surprised. Jack's a hard worker."

Honey's brows rose. "I know that. I didn't think you did."

"Jack and I have an understanding," Jesse said.

"Oh?"

"I told him this morning that I was going to marry you and —"

"You what!" Honey rose from the water like Poseidon in a tempest. Water sluiced down her body, creating jeweled trails over breasts and belly.

Jesse didn't know when he had ever seen her looking more beautiful. Or more angry.

"Now, Honey —"

"Don't you 'Now, Honey' me, you rogue. How could you tell my son such a thing? How could you get his hopes up when you *know* I'm not going to marry you!"

"But you are," Jesse said.

Honey was shivering from cold and trembling with emotion. Jesse took the towel from around his neck and offered it to her. She yanked it out of his hand and wrapped it around herself.

"I'd like to play the gallant and carry you off to the bedroom to make my point, but —" He gestured to the wounded leg and shrugged. "Can't do it."

Honey made a growling sound low in her throat as she marched past Jesse to the bedroom. Actually she had to stop marching long enough to squeeze past him in the doorway, and she had to fight him for the tail end of the towel as she slid by.

"Just have one more little spot I need to wipe," he said, dabbing at his face.

"Let go!" she snapped. She yanked, he pulled, and the ancient terry cloth tore down the middle. "Now look what you've done!"

Tears sprang to Honey's eyes. "You're ruining everything!"

"It's just a towel, Honey," Jesse said, misunderstanding her tears. He tried to follow her into the bedroom, but she shut the door in his face. And locked it.

"Hey, unlock the door."

"Go away, Jesse."

"I thought we were going to talk."

"Go away, Jesse."

"I'm not going to leave, Honey. You might as well open the door."

"Go away, Jesse."

Jesse put a shoulder against the door, just to see how sturdy it was, and concluded that at least the house was well built. His bad leg wouldn't support him if he tried kicking it in. Which was just as well. Honey wasn't likely to be too impressed with that sort of melodrama.

"I'm leaving, Honey," he said.

No answer.

"I said I'm leaving."

Still no answer.

"Aren't you going to say goodbye?"

"Goodbye, Jesse," she sobbed.

"Jeez, Honey. This is stupid. Open the door so we can talk."

She sobbed again.

Jesse's throat constricted. She really sounded upset. Maybe this wasn't the best time to talk to her after all. He had some chores he could do that would keep him busy for a while. Surely she couldn't stay in there all day. He'd catch her when she came down for some coffee later.

Honey heard Jesse's halting step as he limped his way down the stairs. So, he was leaving after all. Honey got into bed and pulled the covers over her head. She didn't want to think about anything. She just wanted to wallow in misery. She should have taken the part of him she could get, the part left over after he'd done his duty to the Rangers. It would have been better than nothing, certainly better than the void he would leave when he was gone.

Then she thought of all the time she would have to spend alone, with no shoulder to share the burden, no lover's ear to hear how the day had gone and offer solace, and her backbone stiffened. She deserved more from a relationship than half measures. She had to accept the fact that Jesse had made his choice.

Honey didn't notice the sun creeping across the sky. She had no knowledge of the fading light at dusk. She never even noticed the sun setting to leave the world in darkness. Her whole life was dark. It couldn't get any blacker.

Meanwhile, Jesse had spent the day waiting patiently for Honey to come to her senses. At noon, he prepared some tomato soup and grilled cheese sandwiches, planning to surprise her with his culinary expertise. He ended up sharing his bounty with Jack, who ate all the sandwiches and dumped the soup with the comment, "Mom makes it better."

When Jesse had explained to Jack that he needed some time alone with Honey, Jack was more than willing to go spend the night with friends again. In fact, Jesse was embarrassed by the lurid grin on the teenager's face when he agreed not to come home too early the next morning.

"Does this mean Mom has agreed to marry you?" Jack asked.

"I haven't quite talked her into it yet," Jesse said.

"But you will."

"I'm sure going to try," Jesse said grimly.

"Don't worry," Jack said, slapping Jesse on the shoulder. "I think Mom loves you."

But as Jesse was discovering, the fact that Honey loved him might not be enough to induce her to marry him. Jack left late in the afternoon. Jesse tiptoed up the stairs and listened by Honey's bedroom door, but there was no sound coming from inside. He decided he was just going to have to outwait her.

It was nearly ten o'clock that evening before he finally decided she wasn't coming out anytime soon. He knocked hard on her bedroom door. "All right, Honey. Enough's enough. Come on out of there so we can talk."

He heard the sound of rustling sheets and then a muffled "Jesse?"

A moment later the door opened. Her hair looked as sleep-tousled as it had the first morning he had come to the Flying Diamond. Her blue eyes were unfocused, confused. She tightened the belt on the man's terry cloth robe she was wearing, then clutched at the top to hold it closed.

"Jesse?" she repeated. "Is that you?"

"Of course it's me. Who did you think it was?"

"I thought you left," she said.

"Why the hell would I do that?" Jesse felt angry and irritable. While he'd been cooling his heels downstairs all day, she'd been up here *sleeping!* "If you're through napping, maybe we could have that talk I mentioned earlier."

"You want to talk?" Honey was still half-asleep.

"Yes, by God, I want to talk! And you're going to listen, do you hear me?" Jesse grabbed hold of her shoulders and shook her for good measure.

The moment Jesse touched her, Honey

came instantly awake. This was no dream. This was no figment of her imagination. A furious Jesse Whitelaw was really shaking the daylights out of her.

"All right, Jesse," she said, putting her hands on his arms to calm him. "I'm ready to listen."

At that moment there was a knock on the kitchen door and a familiar voice called up the stairs, "Honey? Are you home?"

Good old reliable Adam.

Honey ran past Jesse as though he wasn't even there, scrambled down the stairs and met Adam at the door to the kitchen.

He looked tired and frazzled. Honey avoided meeting his eyes, because they still held too much pain.

"I just wanted to let you know that I found some of your stolen cattle on my property," he said. "I'll have some of my cowhands drive them over here tomorrow."

Adam's eyes flickered to a spot behind Honey. "It seems I misjudged you, Whitelaw," Adam said. "I had no idea Chuck Loomis was using my ranch as a base for a statewide rustling operation. I owe you an apology and my thanks." He stuck his hand out to Jesse, who slid a possessive hand around Honey's waist before he reached out to shake it.

Honey felt the tension between the two men. They would never be close friends, but at least they wouldn't be enemies, either.

"I'll be going now," Adam said.

"Are you sure you're all right?" Honey asked.

"My business affairs are in a shambles and I need a new ranch manager, but otherwise I'm fine," Adam said with a self-deprecating smile.

"I'll let you out," Honey said. But when she tried to leave Jesse's side, he tightened his grasp.

Adam saw what was going on and said, "I can see myself out. Goodbye, Honey."

Honey saw from the look on Adam's face that he wouldn't be coming back anytime soon. She felt his sadness, his loneliness. Somewhere out there was a woman who could bring the sparkle back into Adam's life. All Honey had to do was keep her eyes open and help Adam find that special someone.

When the kitchen door closed behind Adam, Jesse took Honey's hand in his and ordered, "Come with me."

He limped his way back up the stairs, down the hall and into her room. Once inside, he turned and locked the door behind them. "I've got something important to say to you, Honey, and it can't wait another minute."

Honey could see Jesse was agitated. While he talked, she led him over to the bed and sat him down. She kneeled to pull off his boots, then lifted his feet up onto the rumpled sheets.

"Are you more comfortable?" she asked.

"Yes. Don't change the subject."

"What is the subject?" Honey asked, climbing into the other side of the bed.

"You're going to marry me, Honey. No ifs, ands, or buts."

"I know," she said.

"No more arguments, no more — What did you say?"

"I said I'll marry you, Jesse."

"But —"

"I shouldn't have tried blackmailing you into quitting your job. I know how much being a Ranger means to you. It isn't fair to ask you to give that up." She smiled. "I'll manage."

Jesse couldn't have loved Honey more than he did in that instant. How brave she was! What strength she possessed! And how she must love him to be willing to make such a concession herself rather than force him to do it. What she couldn't know, what he hadn't realized himself until very recently, was that it was a sacrifice he was willing to make. He loved being a Ranger; he loved Honey more.

Jesse wanted the life she had offered him, a life working side by side with the woman he loved. Raising kids. Running the ranch. Loving Honey.

Jesse swallowed over the lump in his throat. It was hard to speak but he managed, "I love you, Honey." He gently touched her lips with his, revering her, honoring her.

She moved eagerly into his arms, but he held her away.

"There's something I have to tell you," he said.

He saw the anxiety flicker in her eyes and spoke quickly to quell it. "Before I came back here this morning, I resigned from the Texas Rangers."

Honey gasped. "You did? Really?"

"I did. Really."

Honey didn't know what she had done to be rewarded with her heart's desire, but she saw only rainbows on the horizon. Here was a man she could lean on in times of trouble, a man with whom she could share her life, the happiness and sorrow, the good times and the bad.

"I can't believe that this is really happening," Honey said. "Are you sure, Jesse?"

"Sure of what?"

"That you won't be sorry later. That you won't have regrets. That you won't change your mind and —"

"I won't change my mind. I won't have regrets or be sorry. Being a Ranger made it easy to avoid looking at my life as it really is. I've been drifting for years looking for something, Honey. I just didn't know what it was. I've found it here with you and Jack and Jonathan."

"What's that?"

"A place where I can put down roots. A place where my grandchildren can see the fruits of my labor. A home."

Honey didn't know what to say. She felt full. And happy. And by some act of providence she and the man she loved just happened to be in bed together.

"Where's Jack?" she asked.

Jesse grinned. "He's spending the night with a friend."

Honey arched a brow provocatively. "Then we have the whole house to ourselves?"

"Yes, ma'am. We sure do."

"Then I suggest we make use of it."

Jesse arched a questioning brow. "The whole house?"

"Well, we can start in the bedroom. But the desk in the den is nice. There's the kitchen table. And the tub has definite possibilities." Honey laughed at the incredulous look on Jesse's face.

"You'll kill me," he muttered.

"Yeah, but what a way to go," Honey said.

Hours later, Jesse was leaning back in a tubful of steaming water, his nape comfortably settled on the edge of the claw-footed tub. Honey was curled against his chest, her body settled on his lap.

"I didn't think it could be done," he murmured.

"You're a man of many talents, Mr. Whitelaw."

He grinned lazily. "May I return the compliment?"

"Of course." Honey leaned over to lap a drop of water from Jesse's nipple. She felt him stiffen, and gently teased him until his flesh was taut with desire.

Jesse groaned, an animal sound that forced its way past his throat. "Honey," he warned, "you're playing with fire."

She laughed, a sexy sound, and said, "There's plenty of water here if I wanted to put it out . . . which I don't."

A moment later he had turned her to face him, her legs straddling his thighs. He grasped her hips and slowly pulled her down, impaling her.

Honey gasped.

He held her still, trying to gain control of his desire, wanting the pleasure to last. She arched herself against him, forcing him deeper inside the cocoon of wetness and warmth.

"You feel so good, Honey. So damn good."

"May I return the compliment?" she said in a breathless voice. She grasped his shoulders to steady herself as she rocked back and forth, seeking to pleasure him and finding the pleasure given returned tenfold.

Jesse reached out to cup her breasts, to tease the nipples into peaks, to nip and lick and kiss her breasts until Honey was writhing in pleasure. He found the place where their bodies met and teased her until she ached with need. Their mouths joined as his body spilled its seed into hers.

Breathless, Honey sought the solace of his embrace. He held her close as the water lapped in waves against the edge of the tub.

"I can't believe it," she said as he pulled her close and tucked her head beneath his chin. "Oh, the things we can do to improve the ranch! I have so many plans, so many ideas!"

Jesse chuckled. "Whoa, there, woman. One thing at a time."

She looked up at him and grinned. "What shall we do first?"

"First I think we ought to do some planting."

"What are we going to grow?"

"Some hay. Some vegetables. Some babies."

Honey laughed with delight. "Let's start with the babies."

Jesse fell in love all over again. It was amazing how sheer happiness made Honey glow with beauty. His heart felt full. His chest was so tight with feelings it hurt to breathe. He didn't have to drift any longer. He had found his home. Where he would spend each night with his woman. Where he would plant seeds — of many kinds — and watch them grow.

About the Author

Joan Johnston started reading romances to escape the stress of being an attorney with a major national law firm. She soon discovered that writing romances was a lot more fun than writing legal bond indentures. Since then, she has published a number of historical and contemporary category romances. In addition to being an author, Joan is the mother of two children. In her spare time, she enjoys sailing, horseback riding and camping.